A FINE HOW-DO-YOU-DO

"Did you say your name was Skye Fargo? The one they call the Trailsman?"

He started to turn, about to acknowledge the name that had been hung on him, when he saw the smoky light from the lanterns hung around the tent glinting on the blade of a knife coming at his throat.

Fargo's instincts took over, throwing him to the side so that the knife passed harmlessly by his shoulder. The miss threw the man wielding it off-balance. As he struggled to catch himself and bring the blade around in a backhand slash, Fargo drove an elbow into the side of his head. The man went down as people yelled and got out of his way.

The heel of one of Fargo's high-topped boots came down on the wrist of the man's knife hand, pinning it to the hard-packed dirt floor. Fargo bent over and plucked the knife from the man's fingers.

Straightening, Fargo palmed out his Colt and covered the man on the ground. "That was a mighty unfriendly thing to do," he said.

THE
TRAILSMAN
#279

DEATH
VALLEY
VENGEANCE

by

Jon Sharpe

Ⓞ
A SIGNET BOOK

SIGNET
Published by New American Library, a division of
Penguin Group (USA) Inc., 375 Hudson Street,
New York, New York 10014, USA
Penguin Group (Canada), 10 Alcorn Avenue, Toronto,
Ontario M4V 3B2, Canada (a division of Pearson Penguin Canada Inc.)
Penguin Books Ltd., 80 Strand, London WC2R 0RL, England
Penguin Ireland, 25 St. Stephen's Green, Dublin 2,
Ireland (a division of Penguin Books Ltd.)
Penguin Group (Australia), 250 Camberwell Road, Camberwell, Victoria 3124,
Australia (a division of Pearson Australia Group Pty. Ltd.)
Penguin Books India Pvt. Ltd., 11 Community Centre, Panchsheel Park,
New Delhi - 110 017, India
Penguin Group (NZ), Cnr Airborne and Rosedale Roads, Albany,
Auckland 1310, New Zealand (a division of Pearson New Zealand Ltd.)
Penguin Books (South Africa) (Pty.) Ltd., 24 Sturdee Avenue,
Rosebank, Johannesburg 2196, South Africa

Penguin Books Ltd., Registered Offices:
80 Strand, London WC2R 0RL, England

First published by Signet, an imprint of New American Library,
a division of Penguin Group (USA) Inc.

First Printing, January 2005
10 9 8 7 6 5 4 3 2 1

The first chapter of this volume originally appeared in *Mountain Manhunt*,
the two hundred seventy-eighth volume in this series.

 REGISTERED TRADEMARK—MARCA REGISTRADA

Printed in the United States of America

PUBLISHER'S NOTE
This is a work of fiction. Names, characters, places, and incidents either are
the product of the author's imagination or are used fictitiously, and any
resemblance to actual persons, living or dead, events, or locales is entirely
coincidental.

The Trailsman

Beginnings . . . they bend the tree and they mark the man. Skye Fargo was born when he was eighteen. Terror was his midwife, vengeance his first cry. Killing spawned Skye Fargo, ruthless, cold-blooded murder. Out of the acrid smoke of gunpowder still hanging in the air, he rose, cried out a promise never forgotten.

The Trailsman they began to call him all across the West: searcher, scout, hunter, the man who could see where others only looked, his skills for hire but not his soul, the man who lived each day to the fullest, yet trailed each tomorrow. Skye Fargo, the Trailsman, the seeker who could take the wildness of a land and the wanting of a woman and make them his own.

Death Valley, 1860—
a landscape halfway to hell,
where some are as wicked as the devil

1

The big man in buckskins rode down the single street of the mining camp. His lake-blue eyes were alert for trouble. These boom camps were known for sudden outbreaks of violence, and Skye Fargo didn't figure this one would be any exception.

He reined the magnificent black-and-white Ovaro stallion to a halt in front of a sprawling tent saloon. It was early evening, with the red glow of the recently departed sun still in the sky above the Panamint Mountains to the west, but the saloon was already doing a bustling business.

Fargo swung down out of the saddle and with an outstretched hand stopped one of the prospectors hurrying toward the saloon.

"Pardon me, friend," Fargo said. "Does this settlement have a name?"

The man paused but licked his lips impatiently as he glanced toward the tent saloon. "Blackwater, they call it," he replied. "After Blackwater Wash."

Fargo nodded and said, "Obliged." He let the prospector hurry on into the saloon to get on with his drinking.

Instead of going inside himself, Fargo led the stallion on down the street toward a corral made of pine poles cut from the trees that grew higher up on the slopes of the mountains. A much smaller tent sat in front of the corral, and a man perched in front of the tent on a three-legged stool, sipping from a cup of coffee. He nodded pleasantly as Fargo walked up.

"Evenin', mister. Somethin' I can do for you?"

Fargo patted the Ovaro's shoulder. "I'd like to put my horse up for the night."

The man looked at the stallion and let out a low whistle of admiration. "That's one fine piece of horseflesh, mister," he said. "It'd be an honor to have him in my corral. Cost you four bits, though, honor or not."

"That include a rubdown and some grain and water?"

"Sure." The man stood up and moved closer.

"Careful," Fargo advised. "Let him get used to you while I'm still here. Otherwise he's a mite touchy."

"One-man horse, eh?" The corral owner reached out, let the Ovaro smell his hand, and then rubbed the horse's nose. "Seems to take to me all right."

"He can usually tell when somebody's friendly." Fargo handed over the reins. "I reckon you stay close by all night?"

"Right there in that tent. If you're worried about horse thieves, mister, there ain't no need. Most of the men around here are a lot more interested in gold and silver than they are in horses. This is probably the finest animal I've ever seen in Blackwater, but I'll bet not half a dozen fellas even noticed that when you rode into town."

Fargo nodded. "That's all right with me." He wasn't looking to attract any attention.

He had come to Blackwater on business, though, and now he was ready to get on with it. He gave the corral man a couple of coins, then walked back down the street to the saloon.

The only sign in front of the place consisted of a couple of boards nailed together in a cross shape and hammered into the ground. The word *whiskey* was hand-lettered on the crosspiece. Paint had run down from the letters and dried.

Fargo pushed back the canvas flap over the entrance and stepped inside. The saloon was crowded and noisy, the air blue-hazed with smoke. Rough planks laid across barrels formed the bar. Men lined up in front of it for drinks. Poker games went on at a few crudely made tables.

Fargo had seen similar places dozens of times in his travels across the West. In the little more than ten years since the discovery of gold at Sutter's Mill, mining camps had sprung up all over California and in other states and territories, too. Fargo had visited many of them.

Not because he was a prospector, however. He had done some mining in his time, but that wasn't what drove him. He was more of a drifter, a man who had a talent for finding and following trails that was unsurpassed on the frontier. He had scouted for the army, guided wagon trains, and taken other jobs that involved following or blazing trails.

Now he had come to Blackwater because someone had gotten word to him through an army colonel he knew, asking Fargo to meet him here and promising a payment of three hundred dollars just to listen to a proposition. Fargo was willing to invest the time it had taken to get here. He hadn't had anything better to do at the moment.

Even though he enjoyed a good game of poker, he wasn't interested in cards right now. Whiskey was a different story. He could use something to cut the dust after the long, dry ride. He headed toward the bar, threading his way through the crowd.

It was late spring, and already the temperatures on the broad salt flat east of the Panamints known as Death Valley were approaching one hundred degrees during the days. At night, though, the air cooled off rapidly and could be downright cold. At the moment it wasn't too bad, dry but not unpleasant. The wind was from the west, carrying the stink of the salt flats away from the settlement.

When Fargo finally edged up to the bar, he found himself facing a burly, red-faced bartender with sweeping mustaches. "What can I do you for, friend?" the man wanted to know.

"Whiskey," Fargo said, and remembering that bartenders were usually the best source of information in a town, he added, "I'm looking for a gent named Slauson. Know him?"

"Can't say as I do," the bartender replied as he splashed liquor from a bottle into a smudged glass. He shoved the glass across the plank bar. "That'll be a dollar."

Fargo thought the price was a mite high but didn't complain. Prices were always high in mining camps. That was just part of the boom. He handed over a coin and tossed back the drink. The whiskey was rotgut, but it cut the dust.

"No idea where I can find the man I'm looking for?"

The bartender shook his head. "Another?"

"No, thanks." The letter Fargo had gotten had specified a meeting here, but that didn't mean the mysterious J. N. Slauson had informed any of the locals about it. Slauson might have Fargo's description and be planning on approaching him, given time. The letter had said to be here if possible sometime during the last two weeks of May, and today's date was May 20.

Fargo turned away from the bar, intending to drift around the room and let himself be seen if anybody was looking for him. It occurred to him that the whole thing might be a trap—there were people who would like nothing better than to see him dead—but he was willing to risk it.

He had taken only a few steps when someone ran

4

into him heavily from the side. "Hey!" a rough voice exclaimed. "Watch where you're goin', damn it!"

"You ran into me," Fargo pointed out as he faced a tall, brawny man in a battered old hat. The man's dark beard was liberally laced with gray.

"The hell I did!" the man said angrily. He lifted knobby-knuckled fists.

Trap, a small voice said again in the back of Fargo's head. And he had walked right into it.

Before the angry prospector could swing at Fargo, though, another voice said sharply, "Gyp, what are you doing?"

The man looked around with a frown and said, "This fella ran into me!"

"Are you sure about that?" A much smaller man stepped up beside him and continued in a reasonable voice. "You know you have a habit of not watching where you're going. Is it possible you ran into him?"

The big man snatched his hat off and scratched at the thatch of graying dark hair on his head. "Well, yeah, I reckon it's possible," he said reluctantly.

"Then you shouldn't try to hit him," the smaller man said. "In fact, you should probably apologize."

"Do I gotta?"

The smaller man sighed. "It would be the polite thing to do."

"Well . . . all right." The big man turned back to Fargo and stuck out a grimy paw. "I'm sorry, mister. I didn't mean to start no trouble."

"That's all right," Fargo told him as he shook hands. He looked at the smaller man, who was also dressed like a prospector in well-worn but neat overalls, a flannel shirt, and a bowler hat that was pushed back to reveal thinning sandy hair.

"My friend here is Gypsum Dailey," the man introduced himself. "My name is Frank Jordan."

Fargo shook hands with him as well. "Skye Fargo."

5

The big man laughed and said, "Frank says I should have been a confidence man, 'cause I got the right name for it. Gyp Some Daily—you get it?"

Fargo smiled and nodded. Clearly, this was an accidental encounter after all, and not a trap as he had suspected for a moment.

"They just call me that, though, on account of I used to work in a gypsum mine."

"Makes sense," Fargo said with a nod. He got the impression that Gypsum Dailey was a little slow in the head. Maybe that was why Frank Jordan had partnered up with him, to sort of look out for him. And as big as Gypsum was, he would be a good worker to have around a mining claim, too.

Jordan said, "Can we buy you a drink, Mr. Fargo, to maybe make up for that little unpleasantness?"

Fargo shook his head. "No need for that. Your friend didn't cause any harm."

"You're sure?"

Fargo nodded. "I appreciate the offer, anyway."

"All right, then." Jordan put a hand on Gypsum's arm. "Come on, we need to head back to the claim before it gets too much later."

"Sure." Gypsum lifted a hamlike hand in farewell. "Be seein' you, mister," he said to Fargo.

Fargo gave the men a friendly nod and watched as they made their way to the saloon's entrance and stepped outside. He was about to move over and watch a few hands in one of the poker games when a voice said behind him, "Did you say your name was Skye Fargo? The one they call the Trailsman?"

He started to turn, about to acknowledge the name that had been hung on him, when he saw the smoky light from the lanterns hung around the tent glinting on the blade of a knife coming at his throat.

Fargo's instincts took over, throwing him to the side so that the knife passed harmlessly by his shoulder. The miss threw the man wielding it off-balance.

As he struggled to catch himself and bring the blade around in a backhand slash, Fargo drove an elbow into the side of his head. The man went down as people yelled and got out of his way.

The heel of one of Fargo's high-topped boots came down on the wrist of the man's knife hand, pinning it to the hard-packed dirt floor. Fargo bent over and plucked the knife from the man's fingers.

Straightening, Fargo palmed out his Colt and covered the man on the ground. "That was a mighty unfriendly thing to do," he said.

The man was a stranger to Fargo. Young, rat-faced, and dirty, he looked like a typical hardcase. He stared wide-eyed at the muzzle of the revolver in Fargo's hand, then swallowed and said, "Go ahead, shoot me. Kill me just like you killed my brother, you son of a bitch."

Fargo shook his head. "I don't know you. Who was your brother?"

"Arnie Tyler. You shot him in Santa Fe last year."

"Sorry, I don't recollect who you're talking about. If I shot your brother, though, I reckon he must've tried to shoot me first."

The young man sneered. "Yeah, that'd be your story, all right. Big hero. But you're really nothin' but a murderin' bastard."

Fargo was getting a little weary of this youngster's abuse. He said, "If I was a murderer, I wouldn't think twice about blowing your head off right now, would I?"

He looked around at the saloon's other customers. They had fallen silent and were watching to see how this drama was going to play out.

"Any law in this settlement?" Fargo asked.

"None to speak of, mister," the bartender called over from behind the planks. "Deputy from the county seat gets by here maybe once a month."

Another man spoke up, saying, "Nobody would

7

think much of it if you were to go ahead and shoot this young scoundrel, mister. We all saw him take that knife after you."

The young man's eyes widened a little more. Clearly he expected Fargo to fire at any moment.

Instead, Fargo stepped back and holstered the Colt. He said, "Stand up and get out of here. I'll leave your knife with the bartender. You can come back and get it later, when I'm not here."

"You . . . you're not gonna shoot me?"

"Nope. Not unless you're an idiot and want to push this farther. I'm sorry your brother's dead, but I don't make a habit of shooting people unless they leave me no other choice."

The youngster rolled over, pushed himself up on hands and knees, and then came to his feet. He cast a furtive glare at Fargo and shuffled toward the entrance, muttering under his breath as he went. He slapped the canvas aside and disappeared into the night.

Fargo hoped he hadn't made a mistake by letting him go. He would have to watch his back while he was here in Blackwater.

But then, he did that all the time anyway, since he was sort of fond of staying alive.

Shaking his head, he started toward the bar. He had decided that another drink didn't sound like such a bad idea after all. The noise level in the saloon went back up, now that it was obvious there wasn't going to be any gunplay, at least not right away.

The bartender already had a shot poured when Fargo got there. He pushed it across the bar and said, "Here you go. Figured you'd be wantin' it."

Fargo tossed back the drink and felt the warm glow the whiskey started in his belly.

"You seem to attract trouble, mister," the bartender went on. "Of course, that ain't hard to do where ol' Gyp is concerned. He'd get into a brawl every night if he didn't have Frank around to look after him."

"Troublesome, is he?"

"He's just not quite right upstairs. The way I heard the story, he used to be as smart as anybody else, but then he got caught in a mine cave-in and one of the beams hit him in the head. When they pulled him out, they didn't even think he'd live. He did, but he was never the same."

"That's a shame," Fargo said. He had heard of other men who had been damaged like that from being hit in the head.

"And that kid," the bartender went on, "he's just a little rat, just like he looks. It's been suspected he's a thief, but nobody's caught him with the proof yet. He'll get strung up sooner or later, though. I'd bet on that."

"No bet," Fargo said. He suspected the youngster would come to a bad end, too.

"Sorry I can't help you with that fella you're looking for. Slauson, was that the name?"

Fargo nodded.

"Friend of yours?"

"Never met the man before," Fargo said. "He sent me a letter asking me to meet him here. Said he had a business proposition for me."

"Well, if I happen to run into him, I'll let him know you're around."

"Much obliged." Fargo put his hand over his glass as the bartender lifted the bottle, offering him another drink. "I don't suppose a fella could rent a place to sleep around here?"

"Head on down the street a ways and you'll come to another big tent. The man who owns it rents out cots. It's expensive, and it ain't all that comfortable from what I've heard, but it beats sleeping on the ground."

Fargo wasn't so sure of that. He had spent plenty

of nights with his blankets spread out on the ground with a bed of pine needles under them, and he usually slept well.

But this was arid country where the settlement was located, with only scrub brush around. The pines grew higher on the slopes. He would see about renting one of those cots and give it a try.

He left the saloon tent and walked down the street. His path took him past the corral where he had left the Ovaro. The owner still sat in front of his tent, smoking a pipe now. He gave Fargo a friendly nod.

"I took good care of that stallion of yours," he said. "Care to have a look at him?"

"I can see him there in the corral," Fargo replied. There was enough light from the moon and stars for him to pick out the sleek-muscled black-and-white form. Since the corral owner seemed friendly, Fargo asked him, "Do you happen to know a gent named Slauson? J. N. Slauson?"

"Can't say as I do. Friend of yours?"

Fargo didn't want to go through the whole thing again, so he said, "Just a man I'm supposed to meet here in this settlement."

"Good luck." The man waved his pipe at the crowded street. "As you can see, there are plenty of men here."

"All after gold and silver."

"Yep. The lure of precious metals."

"Have there been any big strikes?" Fargo asked.

The corral owner shook his head. "No, but a few claims have paid off nicely. Well enough to keep the boom going, anyway."

"You do any prospecting yourself?"

The man laughed. "I came out here to California in forty-nine, me and a few other fellas. You may have heard about it."

"Seems like I did," Fargo said dryly.

"I busted my back leaning over a creek panning

for gold. Never did find much. But I followed it from strike to strike, boomtown to boomtown, until I didn't know how to do much of anything else. Finally decided I'd let the other fella bust his back, though, and find some other way of making a living." He pointed the stem of the pipe at the corral. "This is it."

"Well, I hope it works out for you."

"And I hope you find who you're looking for."

With a nod, Fargo walked on down the street. He saw a large tent looming up on the right. That had to be the place the bartender had told him about. There wasn't another tent that size at this end of the settlement.

Before he could get there, a foot scuffed in the dirt behind him. Instantly, Fargo tensed and swung around, his hand going to the butt of his Colt. He saw a figure step toward him, but the move wasn't threatening.

Something about the shape of the person approaching him kept him from pulling his iron, too. He realized with a little shock that he was looking at feminine curves. So far he hadn't seen even one woman in Blackwater, not even a soiled dove in the saloon.

"Mr. Fargo?" The voice was low and controlled, just husky enough to give the words a slightly sensual edge.

"That's right," Fargo said. He kept his right hand near the butt of the Colt. From time to time in the past, women had tried to kill him. A female finger could pull a trigger just like a man's could.

"I'm Julia Slauson."

Fargo took a sharply indrawn breath of surprise. "I'm supposed to meet a man named J. N. Slauson."

"No, you're supposed to meet me . . . Julia Nicole Slauson."

Fargo thought back to the note he had received

11

from the army officer, passing along the message. "Colonel Price didn't say anything about you being a woman."

"The colonel and my father served together during the Mexican War," Julia Nicole Slauson said. "My father saved Colonel Price's life at Vera Cruz. He was willing to do a favor for me, especially since my father is involved in the trouble I need your help with."

Despite a touch of irritation at being lied to, at least by omission, Fargo felt a quickening of interest at the mention of trouble. He enjoyed listening to Julia talk, too. He found the slightly husky sound of her voice very appealing.

And from what he could see in the shadows, the curves of her body were a mite interesting, too. Fargo had a great appreciation for a handsome woman.

"I reckon we can discuss the situation," he said.

"I was hoping you'd feel that way."

"We can go back down to the saloon—"

"I'd rather not," Julia said. "The men in there, well, most of them haven't seen a woman in quite a while. I know they mean no harm, but the attention makes me feel a little uncomfortable."

"All right. Where do you suggest we talk?"

"I have a wagon . . ."

She didn't want to go into the saloon, Fargo thought, but she didn't mind the idea of being alone in a wagon with a strange man. Well, if she didn't mind the impropriety, he sure didn't either.

"Let's go."

She led the way along the street to a good-sized wagon. The bed had an arching canvas cover on it. She didn't ask him to come inside but rather she sat on the lowered tailgate. Fargo stood in front of her.

"I'm afraid I don't have any coffee or anything like that to offer you."

12

"Don't worry about that," he said. "Just tell me what's wrong."

"You'll want your money, I suppose. What I promised you for meeting me here, I mean."

"That can wait," Fargo told her, sensing that she was stalling a little now that the time had come to explain. Right now he was more interested in her story than in the promised payoff.

"All right." Julia took a deep breath. "Colonel Price told me that you're the best man he's ever seen at finding someone."

"I've tracked down a few folks," Fargo admitted.

"I want you to look for my father."

"He's disappeared?"

Julia waved her hand to the east, the gesture taking in the vast sweep of salt flats known as Death Valley, as well as the stark, stony mountain ranges that bordered it.

"He's out there somewhere," she said, her voice a little hollow with strain. "He came to find his fortune, but I'm afraid he hasn't found anything but trouble."

"Doing some prospecting, is he?"

"That's right. After he left the army, he tried to start a freighting business, but it failed. A few more ventures were equally unsuccessful. As long as my mother was alive, she . . . she kept his spirits up. But after she passed away last year, he became . . . obsessed, I guess you would say, with getting rich."

"Prospecting is one way of doing that . . . for a very lucky few," Fargo said.

Julia nodded. "I realize that. I knew the odds were against him. But it seemed to be so important to him that I urged him to go ahead. Now I wish I hadn't."

"How long has it been since you heard from him?"

"Six months."

Fargo frowned. "That's really not that long, considering where he went. It's not like you can send a letter just anywhere in Death Valley. In fact, the nearest post office is probably more than a hundred miles from here."

"I know that. And normally, while I'd be worried about him, I wouldn't have come out here myself and asked you to meet me here."

"So what happened to change that?" Fargo asked.

"A man came to see me in Los Angeles—that's where I was staying while my father was on this prospecting trip—and said he was my father's partner. He asked me for money so they could buy more supplies. I . . . I thought there was something odd about it."

"You were wise to think that," Fargo told her. "He was probably just trying to chisel some money out of you. He might have met your father, but I'd bet they weren't partners."

"That's what I thought. I put the man off. He came to see me at the dress shop where I'd been working, and I told him to come to my room that night."

"I'm not sure that was a good idea," Fargo said.

"I know it wasn't. That night I hid in the alley and watched the boardinghouse where I lived. Several men snuck around to the back. One of them was the man who had come to see me. They had their guns drawn. They went in, and then a moment later I saw the glow of a match through the window of my room. They were looking for me, Mr. Fargo. I'm sure of it."

Fargo nodded, his face grim. "I expect you're right. And it sounds like they didn't mean you any good, either."

"I think they came there to kidnap me," Julia Slauson said calmly.

"Why would they do that?"

"To use me as a weapon against my father. You see, Mr. Fargo, I believe my father must have found

14

a very valuable mine, and these men will stop at nothing to get their hands on it."

That sounded plausible enough, but Fargo pointed out, "You don't have any proof of that."

Julia shook her head. "No, I don't. But I believe it, and I want to get to my father so I can help him."

"You want me to find him and take you to him?"

"That's exactly what I want, Mr. Fargo." She stood up from the tailgate and moved closer to him. Her voice grew more throaty as she went on. "I . . . I have some money and if you help me, I'll do anything you want, Mr. Fargo. Anything at all."

2

Fargo frowned again. "You don't believe in being coy, do you, Miss Slauson?"

She tossed her head, making her thick dark hair swirl around her shoulders. "I was raised to speak my mind," she said with a defiant edge in her voice. "I realize that makes me different from many women, but I can't help it. If my plainspoken ways offend you—"

"I didn't say that," Fargo broke in. "I like it when folks put their cards on the table, male or female."

"Then we should get along just fine. Now, as to my offer—"

Fargo held up a hand to stop her. "We don't have to talk about that now. You've got enough money for supplies?"

"Yes, I do. I brought all of my savings with me."

"I wouldn't go around talking about that if I was you," Fargo advised her.

"I don't intend to, but I assume I can trust you."

"You never met me before tonight."

"No, but . . ." And now her voice broke a little. Fargo recognized it as a sign of the strain she was under. "I have to trust *somebody*, don't I? If I'm going to help my father, I mean."

"All right," Fargo said. "I'll try to find your father. You've got my word on that."

"Colonel Price told me from the beginning that Skye Fargo is a man of his word."

"I try. You can pay for the supplies, and we'll talk about everything else later on, after I've located your father and found out what all this is about."

"You'll take me with you, of course."

Fargo wasn't so sure about that, and he said as much. "Death Valley is a dangerous place," he told Julia. "Folks have gone in there and never come back out."

"Do you honestly think I'd be safer here in Blackwater?" she asked.

Fargo thought about that for a moment. Most of the time, no matter how rough the surroundings, a decent woman was indeed safe on the frontier. Any man who bothered her would find himself tarred and feathered and run out of town on a rail, if he was lucky. If he wasn't lucky, he might be strung up from the nearest tree.

But as Julia herself had pointed out, most of these prospectors hadn't seen a woman for a long time. The temptation might be too much for them, even knowing what fate could be in store for them. She was right—it would be dangerous for her to remain in Blackwater while Fargo searched for her father.

But would it be even more dangerous for her to venture into Death Valley with him? Fargo didn't know the answer to that.

"We'll hash it out in the morning," he said. "That's when we'll round up the supplies, too."

"All right. But I *am* going."

Fargo didn't waste his breath arguing with her. Let her be stubborn tonight, he thought. Tomorrow might be different.

"I'll be staying here in my wagon," Julia went on. "I've been here for several nights, and no one has bothered me . . . yet. I keep a loaded pistol close at all times, though."

"You know how to use it?"

"My father was an army officer, remember? He made sure I could handle a gun, even though my mother thought it was scandalous and very unlady-like."

Fargo couldn't help but grin. "Sounds like your pa was trying to raise a boy and a girl at the same time."

"Wait until you see me ride."

Fargo didn't rise to that bait. He just nodded and said, "I'll get my bedroll and pitch it under the wagon. I was going to rent a cot for the night, but I think this'll be better."

"I can take care of myself—" she began.

"Have you seen any more of the man who visited you in Los Angeles?"

She shook her head. "No. I left town that very night, and I think I gave him and his companions the slip. I haven't seen them since."

Fargo raked a thumbnail along his jawline with its closely cropped black beard. "If they want to get their hands on you," he mused, "they're liable to follow you here and try again. I'll feel better if I stick close to you."

"All the more reason to take me with you when you start searching for my father."

Fargo grinned. That was a point in favor of her argument, all right.

"Go on and get inside the wagon," he told her. "If anybody tries to climb in, use your gun and venti-late him."

"What if it's you?"

"I won't be climbing in there," Fargo said.

"Not ever?"

"Not tonight," Fargo said. Let her make of that what she would.

There were a couple of cafés in Blackwater, neither of them too clean or appetizing, but Fargo and Julia picked the better of the two for breakfast the next morning. While they sipped coffee and waited for their food, Fargo asked, "Is the team that pulls your wagon horses or mules?"

"Mules," Julia replied. "I bought them along with the wagon in Los Angeles."

"And drove up here all by yourself?"

She shrugged. "I didn't have any trouble. But if I had, there was a shotgun in the wagon, as well as my pistol."

Fargo grinned over his coffee cup. "You pack a lot of iron for a woman."

"I won't be taken advantage of simply because of my sex," she said with a frown.

"No reason to be," Fargo returned easily. He steered the conversation back where it had been headed by saying, "It's a good thing you've got mules. They're better for traveling in rugged country. And you won't find country much more rugged than this around here."

"No, you won't," she agreed. "It has a certain stark beauty, though, don't you think?"

Fargo grunted. "For about ten minutes. Then it's just flat and dry and hot and desolate."

"Yes, I suppose so. What supplies do we need?"

For a few minutes they talked about provisions, and then their plates of flapjacks and bacon arrived at the table, carried by a waiter in a dirty apron. They dug in, and despite the surroundings, the food wasn't too bad. It was almost good, in fact.

"I saw an emporium back up the street," Fargo said as they were eating. "We'll stock up there and then get started."

"You mean for us to leave today?"

"No reason to wait, is there?"

Julia shook her head. "None at all. I'd rather get started. The longer it is before we find my father, the greater the chance that something might happen to

19

him." She paused, then added, "I'm glad you're being reasonable about taking me along."

"I'm still not sure it's the right thing to do. But I figure I'd rather have you where I can keep an eye on you than have to be worrying about you all the time."

"We still haven't discussed your payment—"

Fargo held up a hand to stop her. "Right now you need to use the money you have for supplies. There'll be time enough to talk about the other later."

"All right." She looked at him levelly across the table, and he saw that her eyes were a deep, rich brown. "I meant what I said, though. Remember that."

Fargo gave a curt nod, thinking that it wasn't likely he was going to forget.

They finished their breakfast and left the café. Fargo asked, "Where are the mules?"

Julia pointed. "Over there in the corral."

It was the same place where Fargo had left his Ovaro for the night. "I'll get them and lead them down to your wagon so I can start hitching them up," he said. "You go on to the store and see about the supplies. I'll be along directly."

"You think it's safe for us to split up?"

Fargo glanced around. The camp wasn't nearly as busy as it had been the night before. The prospectors who had clogged the single street were back up in the fan-shaped hills, either working their claims or searching for new ones. But there were still quite a few people around.

"You have your gun?" he asked.

Julia slipped her hand into a pocket in her dress. "I try to keep it with me as much as I can."

Fargo nodded. "All right, then. I don't think anybody's going to try to bother you in broad daylight, but if they do, fire a shot and I'll come a-runnin'."

"If I have to fire a shot, I intend to aim it at whoever's bothering me."

"Then I'll come along and haul off the body," Fargo said with a grin.

He left Julia there and headed over to the corral, thinking as he did so that she was one of the feistiest young women he had run into lately. Beautiful, too, with that thick dark hair, those brown eyes, and a tiny dimple in the middle of her defiant chin.

She had made it pretty plain once again this morning that she wouldn't have any objection to going to bed with him. Fargo had a feeling she would be an inventive, enthusiastic partner if they ever did wind up sharing some blankets.

The problem was that Julia was still using that to barter with him, and Fargo didn't care for that attitude. When he made love with a woman, he wanted it to be for the sheer joy of the experience for both of them, not because she felt like she owed him something. Maybe, once he and Julia knew each other a little better, things would be different.

What she didn't know was that he would have helped her find her father simply as a favor to her, and to his friend Colonel Price. Loyalty meant a great deal to Skye Fargo, and so did justice. He never refused help to someone who deserved it.

The proprietor of the corral greeted him with a grin. The man stood by the pine pole fence, a steaming cup of coffee in his hand. He had built a little campfire by his tent, and he had bacon sizzling in a pan.

"Howdy," he said. "Had breakfast yet?"

"As a matter of fact, I have," Fargo replied. "I think what you're fixing up there will be better, though."

"You're welcome to share."

Fargo shook his head. "No, thanks."

"Come to pick up that fine horse o' yours?"

"That's right, along with Miss Slauson's mule team."

"Slauson?" the man repeated. "I thought you were looking for a fella named Slauson."

"I thought so, too. Turned out I was wrong," Fargo said dryly.

"I know the mules you're talking about. They belong to that pretty young lady who came into camp in a wagon a few days ago. She never told me her name, though, or I sure wouldn't have told you I didn't know anybody named Slauson."

"Don't worry about it," Fargo assured him. "She found me just fine."

"The two of you goin' someplace together?"

Fargo hesitated. The corral man was friendly, but Fargo didn't really know him. Anyway, he had always played his cards pretty close to the vest, just out of habit, and Fargo didn't see any reason to change now.

"That's right," he said, and left it at that.

The corral man seemed satisfied with the answer. He set his coffee down and said, "I'll help you with the mules."

He and Fargo had just turned toward the pole structure when a man came around the far corner of it. Fargo recognized the young, ratlike face, which was now contorted with hatred and anger.

"Now you'll get what's comin' to you, Fargo!" the man cried as he jerked up the double-barreled shotgun in his hands.

The range was about twenty feet. At that distance, the charges in the Greener's twin barrels would blow apart not only Fargo but also the corral man beside him. Fargo's hand dipped toward the Colt on his hip. Two lives rode on the speed of his draw.

Fargo's hand moved almost too fast for the eye to follow. The revolver came smoothly out of leather. The barrel tipped up as Fargo's thumb drew back the hammer, and then flame gouted from the muzzle as the Colt roared.

The bullet smacked cleanly into the chest of the man wielding the shotgun and knocked him backward. The barrels of the scattergun pointed skyward as he involuntarily jerked the triggers. With a pair of dull booms, the shotgun sent its charges of buckshot harmlessly into the air.

A moment later, as smoke still curled from the barrel of Fargo's Colt, the buckshot pattered back down like leaden rain.

Fargo stalked forward, keeping his gun trained on the fallen man just in case he had another weapon. The rat-faced would-be killer wasn't in any shape to pose a threat, though. He pawed at the hole in his chest that welled blood. His back arched as the heels of his boots scratched futilely in the street.

The young man looked up at Fargo. Blood trickled from the corner of his mouth. "I got . . . I got another brother!" he gasped. "He'll settle with you . . . you bastard! You've killed me!"

"What's your name?" Fargo asked. He knew the young man's last name was Tyler, but he figured he ought to know the front handle, too, so he could tell whoever was in charge of burying around here what to put on the marker.

"J-Jonah . . . Jonah Tyler."

"I wish you hadn't made me shoot you, Jonah Tyler," Fargo said, but by that time it was too late. Ratface was beyond hearing him.

Fargo shook his head and holstered the Colt after reloading the chamber he had emptied. The corral man came up beside him. A few other bystanders who had been drawn by the shots stood a short distance off, watching.

"Reckon you just saved my life," the corral man said. "That Greener would've blown the hell out of both of us if it had gone off while it was pointed in our direction. I never saw a draw quite so fast."

"Nothing makes a fella move like the imminent

23

prospect of having his head blown off," Fargo said with a humorless smile.

"Well, the kid was asking for it, that's for damned sure. What was that he said about having a brother?"

"According to him, I killed his brother last year," Fargo explained. "We had a run-in at the saloon last night when he tried to take a knife to me."

The corral man rubbed his beard-stubbled jaw. "Yeah, I think I heard some gents talking about that."

"Evidently he has another brother, and that one's going to be coming after me, too."

"I don't think I'd want the sort of enemies you seem to have, Mr. Fargo."

Fargo didn't necessarily want them, either, but the way trouble followed him around, he didn't seem to have much choice in the matter.

"Mr. Fargo!" a voice called anxiously.

He turned to see Julia Slauson hurrying toward him, a worried look on her face. As she came up to him, she went on. "I heard shooting, and when I stepped out of the store to have a look, I saw you over here with . . . with . . ."

Her eyes cut toward the bloodied body in the street, then looked away. "Are you all right?"

Fargo nodded. "I'm fine. How are you coming with those supplies?"

She glanced at the corpse again, as if surprised that he could be so calm under the circumstances, then said, "The clerk had just started gathering them for me."

"Go on back over there and I'll see you in a few minutes."

"All right." She hesitated. "This . . . this shooting didn't have anything to do with . . ."

"It was strictly a personal grudge," Fargo assured her.

She nodded and went back to the store, but she

threw a glance or two over her shoulder along the way.

"We ain't never been properly introduced," the corral man said as he put out his hand to Fargo. "My name's Dale Wiley. Figured you ought to know it, seeing as how you saved my life and all."

"Glad to meet you, Dale," Fargo said as he shook Wiley's hand.

A short, grizzled man in a leather apron and a knitted cap came down the street wheeling a cart. He greeted Fargo and Wiley by saying, "If'n you'll toss the deceased in here, I'll take him off and plant him."

"You're the local undertaker?" Fargo said.

"Close as Blackwater's got, anyway. I do a little barberin', carpentry, odd jobs and such. Anything for a dollar." The man spat in the dust.

"I ain't sure this one's got even a dollar in his pocket, Sanderson," Wiley said.

"Well, whatever he's got, it'll be enough, I reckon. I'd bury him anyway. Somebody's got to."

Fargo took the dead man's shoulders while Wiley got his feet. Together, they lifted him and heaved him into the cart. Sanderson trundled the body away to dispose of it. There wasn't much room for sentiment in a place like Blackwater.

With that unpleasant task taken care of, Fargo and Wiley got hackamores on the mules and led the balky critters out of the corral. Fargo gathered up the reins and said, "I'll go hitch them up, then come back for my stallion."

"Want me to saddle him up for you?" Wiley asked.

Fargo shook his head. "I generally handle that chore myself."

Wiley nodded in understanding. A lot of men preferred to saddle their own horses so that they would know the job had been done right.

Fargo took the mules down the street to Julia's wagon, tugging hard on the reins when they tried to resist. He tied them to one of the wagon wheels, then one by one got them hitched up to the vehicle. When he was done he left them there and returned to the corral.

Wiley was eating breakfast by this point. The bacon had burned a little while he and Fargo were almost getting shot by Jonah Tyler, but it still smelled pretty good, as did the coffee. Fargo wouldn't have minded sipping another cup and shooting the breeze with Wiley for a while, but he had work to do.

When he had the saddle on the Ovaro, he took the stallion down the street and tied him in front of the emporium. The building had a wooden framework, but the sides and roof were made of canvas hastily stretched and nailed onto the boards. It was a fast way to put up a building.

The canvas entrance flap was tied back to let in light and air. Fargo went inside. Just as in the saloon, counters had been set up by laying planks over barrels. Planks and crates formed shelves where canned goods and other supplies were stacked. Fargo spotted Julia in the rear of the place, talking to a clerk.

The counter in front of her was piled high with bags of flour, sugar, beans, and salt; sides of bacon wrapped in oilcloth; boxes of shotgun shells and cartridges for Fargo's Colt and the Henry rifle he carried; canteens, and other assorted items they might need on their trip.

Julia turned to Fargo and asked, "Any more trouble?"

He shook his head. "Nope. The team's hitched up, and my horse is saddled and ready to go."

The young clerk said eagerly, "I'll put all this in a box for you, Miss Slauson."

She gave him a grateful smile. "Thank you."

Fargo waited until the supplies were boxed up,

then lifted the box and carried it out of the emporium. Balancing it on one shoulder, he took the Ovaro's reins in his other hand. Julia walked alongside him.

"Looked like you made a conquest, the way that clerk was grinning at you," Fargo commented.

"Are you jealous, Mr. Fargo?"

"Not particularly. And call me Skye. If we're going to be traveling together we might as well be on good terms."

"Yes, indeed, Skye. And I'm Julia, of course."

Fargo nodded. When they came to the wagon, he placed the box of supplies in the back. By the time he walked to the front, Julia had climbed onto the driver's seat without waiting for any assistance.

"I'm ready," she said as she took up the reins. She had been wearing a bonnet with the strings tied around her neck, but the bonnet itself was pushed back. Now she had pulled it up so that it shielded her head from the sun.

Fargo swung up into the saddle. "Do you have any idea where to start looking for your father?"

"I'm sorry," Julia said with a shake of her head. "All I know is that he came to this area."

Fargo nodded as he thought. "Death Valley runs pretty much north and south. We're close to the north end, on the west side. There's no gold or silver out on the salt flats themselves, so nobody prospects there. The claims are all in the hills bordering the flats on both sides."

He pointed as he talked, indicating where he was talking about. Julia listened with keen interest.

"We'll work our way down the west side, along the Panamints to the Owlshead Mountains at the south end of the valley. Then, if we haven't found your father yet, we'll come back up the other side along the Black Mountains."

"How long will that take?"

"A week, maybe two. We can't push the mules in this weather."

"What about water?"

"There are springs in the hills and some wells along the edges of the salt flats, if you know where to find them. Not all the wells have drinkable water, though. Some of it's too salty. We'll fill all the canteens and our water barrel anytime we find a good supply of freshwater." He pointed across the valley. "There are some big warm springs over there around Furnace Creek. Of course, that's one of the last places we'll get to."

Julia nodded. "You were right. This is going to be a dangerous undertaking, isn't it?"

"We'll be all right," Fargo told her. "It's just a matter of being careful and knowing what you're doing."

"And you know what you're doing, don't you?"

"Most of the time." Fargo lifted the reins and heeled the stallion into motion. "Let's go."

He rode down Blackwater's single street. Julia flapped the reins and shouted at the mules and got them moving after a moment. Fargo paused at the edge of the settlement to wait for her. Then he rode south with the wagon rolling along steadily behind him.

Blackwater, and the wash that had given the camp its name, soon disappeared behind them. The ground was rocky in places, hard-packed dirt and dried, salty hardpan in others. The wagon didn't have much trouble negotiating the terrain.

To Fargo's right were fan-shaped hills that had been formed by rockslides and silt washing down from the Panamint Mountains. The hills were cut by narrow canyons, dry washes, and arroyos that ran water only during the very occasional downpours. It was in those hills, along the canyons and washes, that prospectors searched for pockets of gold and silver.

They would have to check every wash for Julia's father. It would be a tedious, time-consuming job, but Fargo didn't know how else to proceed. They might get lucky and find the elder Slauson in a day or two, or it might be a week or even more before they ran across him—assuming he was even here around Death Valley somewhere.

The air had been a little cool before dawn, but as soon as the brassy red ball peeked over the mountains to the east, it started getting hot. The temperature rose as the sun climbed higher in the sky. By midmorning Fargo was sweating heavily, and when he looked back at Julia, he saw dark stains on her gray dress. Sweat was just something people in these parts had to put up with.

Around noon they reached the first of the canyons that led up into the hills on their right. Fargo called a halt and said, "After we eat a little, we'll have a look up that way."

"It's almost too hot to eat," Julia said. "I'm not even hungry."

"Neither am I, but we'll eat some anyway. Got to keep our strength up."

"We just started," she pointed out.

"This weather will drain a body quicker than you think it will."

Fargo cooked biscuits, making a big enough batch to last for several meals, and he gave Julia some jerky to chew on, too. As she gnawed at the tough, dried strip of meat, she said, "How are you supposed to eat this, anyway?"

"You're doing just fine," Fargo told her with a grin. "After a while, you'll get used to it."

She just shook her head as if that wasn't likely to happen.

When they were done with their simple meal, Fargo poured water in his hat and gave the stallion and each of the mules a drink. Then they headed up the canyon, which was only about fifty yards wide. It ran fairly straight for a few hundred yards but then twisted through the hills so that they couldn't see beyond the bend.

They hadn't gone very far when the hot, still air was suddenly filled with the sound of gunfire, coming from somewhere up the canyon.

3

Fargo reined in and stiffened in the saddle as he heard the banging of pistols, the sharp cracks of a rifle, and the dull booms of a shotgun. It sounded like a small-scale war going on up there, with at least half a dozen different guns involved.

He looked around at Julia, who had pulled the wagon to an abrupt halt, and snapped, "Stay here!"

"Skye—" she began, as if she was going to argue, but it was too late.

Fargo was already galloping up the canyon, pulling the Henry rifle from its saddle boot as he rode.

He didn't like the idea of leaving Julia alone, but he was convinced the shooting wasn't a distraction meant to lure him away from her. Anybody who was burning that much powder was serious about it. Whoever was up the canyon, they were doing their best to kill each other.

Fargo slowed the stallion as he neared the bend. He didn't want to go charging around there and find himself in the middle of a fusillade. As the Ovaro came to a halt, Fargo swung down from the saddle and ran over to the shoulder of rock that jutted out into the canyon where it twisted. He put his back against it, holding the rifle slanted across his chest.

The gunfire hadn't let up any. If anything, it was growing fiercer. Fargo edged his head around the rock and took a gander at what was going on.

He saw two clusters of boulders on opposite sides of the canyon, set at a slight angle to each other. Clouds of gun smoke drifted above the large rocks. Fargo heard the whine of bullets ricocheting. Clearly, two opposing forces were holed up in those boulders, and neither side could get a good shot at the other.

Without knowing what was going on, he could do nothing but wait and watch. After a few moments, during a brief lull in the firing, a man in the boulders on the right side of the canyon bellowed, "Come out and fight in the open, you damn buzzards!"

Fargo's eyes narrowed. The voice was familiar. Unless he was mistaken, it belonged to Gypsum Dailey, the big, simpleminded miner he'd almost come to blows with in the saloon the night before.

Once Gypsum's partner, Frank Jordan, had intervened, the big man had settled down and been reasonably friendly. Fargo wondered if the claim Gypsum and Jordan had been returning to when they left the saloon was located up this canyon.

He had no idea who the men in the other clump of boulders were, but his inclination was to believe that Gypsum and Jordan were the victims here. For one thing, they were defending themselves with a couple of pistols and a shotgun, while the other men were using rifles. And there were at least four of them, probably a couple more, Fargo estimated.

Fargo's sympathies naturally lay with the underdogs, but he didn't want to get mixed up in this fight and risk his life without knowing for sure what was going on. He started to back off, but then he heard Jordan yell, "Look out, Gypsum! They're above us!"

Fargo looked again and saw that a couple of riflemen had somehow gotten onto a ledge that overlooked the boulders where Gypsum and Jordan were forted up. The men began firing down into the rocks, drawing a howl of pain from one of the prospectors.

That did it, Fargo thought. He didn't like bushwhackers. He was going to have to take a hand in this game after all.

He brought the Henry to his shoulder and drew a bead on the two men on the ledge. Elevating his aim a little, he cranked off three fast shots from the repeater. The bullets splattered off the rock wall of the canyon just above their heads. They yelped and scurried for cover, ducking back around a bulge in the rock.

"Look out, Jack!" a man yelled. "Those two desert rats got friends!"

Fargo brought the barrel of the Henry down and thrust it around the bend. He threw three more rounds into the boulders on that side and heard the slugs bouncing around.

"Let's get the hell out of here!"

That cry was taken up by more men. A few moments later, Fargo heard the sudden, unexpected rataplan of hoofbeats. The men who had attacked Gypsum and Jordan—and Fargo was assuming that was what had happened—must have had horses stashed somewhere down the canyon. Now they were galloping away.

Fargo checked the ledge on the other side of the canyon and saw that the two riflemen were nowhere in sight. They had probably climbed back up to wherever they had left their horses.

"Dailey!" Fargo called. "Jordan! You hear me?"

"Who's that?" Gypsum shouted back. "This better not be a damn trick!"

"No trick, Gypsum! It's Skye Fargo! We met in the saloon in Blackwater last night."

He heard the mutter of conversation between the two prospectors but couldn't make out the words. After a minute or two, Gypsum called, "We need help, Mr. Fargo! Frank's hit!"

He sounded scared. That was enough to convince Fargo that he was telling the truth. He didn't figure

Gypsum Dailey was the type to frighten easily, but his friend and partner being wounded would do it.

Fargo still had to worry about Julia, though. He didn't know who the hardcases were who had jumped the two prospectors, but they were still on the loose, and Julia was alone.

"I'll be back in a minute," he called. "Hang on!"

Vaulting into the saddle, he wheeled the Ovaro and galloped toward the mouth of the canyon. When Julia saw him coming, she stood up on the wagon seat. She had the shotgun in her hands.

Fargo reined in and waved an arm over his head, indicating to her that she should drive the wagon on into the canyon. She sat down, placing the shotgun on the floorboard at her feet, and took up the reins. A moment later, she had the wagon rolling toward Fargo.

Fargo turned around and rode back to the bend. This time he rounded it and headed straight for the rocks where he knew he would find Gypsum and Jordan. As the Trailsman approached, Gypsum stepped out from behind a boulder and waved his arms to get Fargo's attention.

"Over here!" he said. "Hurry, Mr. Fargo! Frank's bleedin' bad!"

Fargo dismounted and let the reins trail, knowing the Ovaro wouldn't stray. He followed Gypsum into the rocks.

Frank Jordan sat propped up against one of the boulders. His hat was off, his fair hair was askew, and his right hand clutched his upper left arm. Blood welled between his fingers.

"Looks like you got elected," Fargo said.

"Nominated real good, anyway," Jordan replied. "What are you doing here, Mr. Fargo?"

"That's a long story. Let's have a look at that arm first."

He hunkered next to Jordan and placed the Henry on the ground. Drawing his Arkansas Toothpick from the sheath strapped to his right calf, he cut away the sleeve of Jordan's shirt and laid bare the wound. Blood still ran from both holes in the fleshy part of the prospector's arm.

"I know it'll hurt like blazes, but you'd better try to move it and make sure the bone's not busted," Fargo advised.

"I don't think it is . . ." Jordan gritted his teeth and moved the arm. "You were right about . . . it hurting like blazes. . . . Seems to work, though."

Fargo nodded. "We'll clean it up and bandage it. It'll be stiff and sore for a while, but with any luck it should heal just fine."

The creaking of wagon wheels and the thudding of the mules' hooves sounded nearby. "Somebody else is comin'!" Gypsum exclaimed. Clutching a shotgun, he ran out of the nest of boulders.

"Gypsum, it's all right!" Fargo called after him. "She's with me!" He hoped Gypsum wouldn't get trigger-happy and take a shot at Julia. He was concerned about the opposite happening, too.

He didn't need to be, because a moment later he heard Gypsum say, "It's a girl, Frank! A pretty girl!"

"Well, be a gentleman," Jordan called out to him. "Escort her in here."

Fargo used the sleeve of Jordan's shirt that he had cut off to wipe away as much of the blood as he could. He heard Julia gasp behind him, no doubt startled by the sight of the blood.

Chances were, she would do well to get used to it, Fargo thought.

"What can I do to help?" she asked as she came up beside him.

"Do you have any whiskey in your wagon?"

"No. And we didn't buy any back in Blackwater."

"You need a drink, Mr. Fargo?" Gypsum asked.

Jordan said, "I imagine he wants the whiskey to clean this wound."

Fargo nodded. "That's right. It'll help keep it from festering."

"We got a jug up at our camp," Gypsum said. "You want me to fetch it?"

"How far is the camp?"

"Just a few hundred yards," Jordan supplied the answer. "If somebody will give me a hand, I can make it there."

Fargo agreed that would be all right. He came to his feet and motioned for Gypsum to help Jordan.

Gypsum moved in and lifted his partner as if Jordan weighed no more than a child. With a meaty arm slung around Jordan's waist, Gypsum helped him shuffle along the canyon floor. Fargo and Julia followed, Fargo leading the Ovaro while Julia tugged the mule team along.

The little group went around another bend, and Fargo saw the camp, which consisted of a tent and a small rope corral where four mules were penned up. The tent had been flattened and trampled by the fleeing outlaws. When Jordan saw that, he let out an angry curse.

"Those bastards! Bad enough they had to jump us and try to kill us, and now they wreck our camp, too!"

"Did you know them?" Fargo asked.

"Sure. That was Puma Jack's bunch."

Fargo shook his head. He had never heard of Puma Jack. "Who's that?"

"An outlaw. Him and his gang have been holding up stagecoaches here in California and over in Arizona Territory for the past six or eight months. They're a bad bunch, and they've taken it in their heads that they can use Death Valley as their hideout."

"Considering the amount of law around here, that's probably not a bad idea," Fargo pointed out.

"That doesn't mean we have to like it." Jordan's face was pale and drawn as he limped along, helped by Gypsum. "A lot of the fellas around here are pretty rough, no doubt about that, but they're not desperadoes. We just want to be left alone to prospect in peace. Instead, nobody's safe as long as Puma Jack and his gang are around."

"I wish somebody would do somethin' about 'em," Gypsum said.

Fargo knew the big prospector wasn't subtle enough to be dropping a hint. Gypsum was just expressing an honest opinion. One that Fargo didn't blame him for holding, either.

But he was traipsing along the edge of Death Valley to search for Julia Slauson's father, not to go after some outlaw gang.

"Jack will come to a bad end sooner or later," Jordan said. "Lawbreakers always do."

Fargo knew that wasn't true. Sometimes a bandit or killer got away clean with his misdeeds. But most of the time justice caught up with them.

A couple of short stools had been busted up when the gang stampeded through the camp, too. Jordan sat down gingerly on the ground, and Gypsum said, "I'll see if I can find the jug. It was in the tent."

In that case it was probably broken by now, Fargo told himself. But to his surprise, after a few moments of rooting around in the debris, Gypsum came up with the jug. It didn't appear to have been harmed.

Fargo soaked a rag in the whiskey and used it to clean the rest of the blood away from the bullet hole. Jordan winced in pain as he did so.

"It'll be worse in a minute," Fargo warned him.

"I know. Just do what needs to be done."

Fargo did, holding up the injured arm and pouring the fiery liquor directly into the wound. Jordan gritted his teeth but couldn't hold back a whimper of pain as the whiskey burned through his arm.

Tearing a rag that Gypsum found for him into strips of cloth, Fargo made a couple of pads and then bound them tightly into place over the entrance and exit wounds.

"That ought to have you fixed up," he told Jordan.

The smaller man's head leaned back against the rock behind him. His eyes were closed.

"Thank you," he said. "I appreciate you patching me up, Mr. Fargo." Jordan opened his eyes and looked up at Fargo. "Now you can tell us just how you and your friend happened to come along while Puma Jack and his bunch were trying to kill us."

"Pure coincidence," Fargo said. "We didn't even know your camp was up this canyon. But when we heard the shooting, I figured I'd better have a look."

"That was a stroke of luck for us. The way we were pinned down, Jack and his men would've got us sooner or later. Wouldn't they, Gypsum?"

"No, I'd have shot all of 'em," Gypsum declared. "They're bad men."

Jordan exchanged a glance with Fargo. Gypsum would have tried to defend them, but both Fargo and Jordan knew it would have been a losing battle if Fargo hadn't spooked the outlaws into running.

As it was, the gang had had them outnumbered and probably could have overcome Fargo, too, but they hadn't stuck around to try.

"Well, I'm glad I could be of help, anyway," Fargo said. "Maybe you fellas can help us."

"Anything we can do, we'll be glad to," Jordan assured him.

Fargo inclined his head toward Julia. "We're looking for Miss Slauson's father. He's supposed to be doing some prospecting somewhere around here."

"Slauson, Slauson," Jordan repeated. He looked at Gypsum. "Do we know anybody by that name?"

Gypsum shook his shaggy head. "Not that I recollect, Frank."

"Has he established a claim?" Jordan asked Fargo.

"We don't know. He may have a claim and a permanent camp, or he may still be prospecting in the hills somewhere."

Fargo didn't mention Julia's theory that her father had found a rich claim and that the men who had snuck into her boardinghouse in Los Angeles meant to kidnap her as leverage to get their hands on that claim. They had no proof of that, and he wasn't sure he was completely convinced of it, either.

"I'm sorry," Jordan said. "We just don't know him. We'd help you if we could. But there are a lot of men out here in these canyons and washes looking for gold, and we haven't run into all of them."

Fargo nodded. "I figured as much, but there was a chance."

Jordan looked at Julia and asked, "When was the last time you saw your pa, miss?"

"It was six months ago," she replied.

"That's not too long. The valley is almost a hundred miles from one end to the other, and there are a lot of little canyons. A fella could spend years out here and not cover the whole place, especially if he's taking his time and prospecting."

"I know, but I have . . . other reasons to be worried."

Jordan started to shrug, then stopped as the movement made pain shoot through his arm. Wincing, he said, "That's your business, miss. We'll take your word for it. And we'll keep our eyes open, too, won't we, Gypsum?"

"We sure will," Gypsum agreed without hesitation. "Keep 'em open for what, Frank?"

"Any sign of Miss Slauson's pa."

"Oh." Gypsum shook his head, having already forgotten the earlier conversation. "I don't know any Slauson."

Fargo indulged his curiosity and asked, "Why did Puma Jack's gang jump you boys in the first place?"

"A week or so ago, a couple of those lowlifes showed up and tried to cadge some whiskey and food off of us. I was here by myself at the time. I tried to run them off, but they started pushing me around. They might have killed me if Gypsum hadn't shown up with his scattergun. He got the drop on them and made them drop their guns."

Gypsum grinned. "Tell Mr. Fargo and the lady what I done then."

"Gave those two the thrashing of their lives—that's what you did." Jordan looked at Fargo and went on. "They swore they'd get even with us. I guess that's what they were trying to do today."

"They're liable to be even more upset that the whole gang got scared off," Fargo pointed out.

"There's nothing I can do about that. We're not going to turn tail and run."

Jordan's tone was proud and stubborn, and Fargo knew that arguing with him wouldn't do any good. But he and Julia couldn't stay here and give them a hand, either, if they hoped to find Julia's father.

"Keep your eyes open all the time," he advised. "There's no way of knowing when the gang might come back."

"They won't take us by surprise again," Jordan vowed.

Another thought occurred to Fargo. "When they rode off, it sounded like they headed on up the canyon."

"They did. There's a freshwater spring at the head of the canyon, as well as a trail that leads on up to a pass through the Panamints. It's pretty rugged, but men on horseback can get through if they're careful. The gang uses it as a sort of back door in and out of Death Valley."

"Is there any·chance other prospectors could be farther up the canyon?"

"Like Miss Slauson's father, you mean?" Jordan shook his head. "Gypsum and I were all the way up at the spring just a few days ago, and we didn't see hide nor hair of anybody. I believe we're the only ones looking for gold in this canyon."

"Any luck?" Fargo asked.

"Not so far. But it's only a matter of time. There's a good strike up here, just waiting for us to find it. I can feel it in my bones," Jordan declared.

Fargo didn't say anything. He had known a heap of miners and prospectors, and without fail, all of them felt like they were on the verge of a big strike. All they had to do was keep on looking a little longer, and then they would be rich beyond their wildest dreams. . . .

That was what they thought, anyway. Seldom did it work out that way, however. Most of them scratched along until they either gave up on their dreams or died.

"Why don't you folks stay the night?" Jordan continued. "We'll fix up the camp, and we'd be glad to share what we've got with you."

Fargo shook his head. "No, we're obliged for the offer, but there's plenty of the day left. We ought to be able to get on down to the next canyon and explore it either this afternoon or in the morning."

"You're sure?"

Fargo glanced at Julia. The lines of strain on her face told him she was anxious to resume the search for her father.

"We're sure," he said.

Jordan struggled to his feet and held out his hand. "Well, then, good luck to you." After shaking hands with Fargo, he shook with Julia as well. "If we run across your pa, miss, or hear anything about him, we'll do our best to get word to you."

"Thank you, Mr. Jordan," she said. "Are you sure you'll be all right?"

"Don't worry about this ventilated wing of mine. Mr. Fargo did a good job on it, and Gypsum can look after me."

"Shoot," Gypsum said, looking down at the ground, "you're the one who looks after me, Frank."

"We'll just take care of each other," Jordan said with a smile.

Fargo helped Julia onto the wagon seat and then mounted the stallion. With a wave of farewell to the two prospectors, he led the way back out of the canyon.

"What's wrong with the one called Gypsum?" Julia asked when they were well out of earshot and heading south, with Fargo riding alongside the wagon.

Fargo shook his head. "I don't know exactly. He was injured in a mine cave-in, and it affected his thinking. He still seems like a pretty good fella, though."

"Yes, he struck me as being rather sweet," Julia said with a smile. "Although I imagine he could be pretty fierce if he was angry, considering how big he is."

"It'd probably be wise not to get him riled up, all right," Fargo allowed dryly.

They followed the hills on down the western edge of Death Valley, until late in the afternoon when they came to the next main canyon that branched off. During the afternoon they had passed several smaller canyons and washes, but those had run only a few hundred yards back into the hills before petering out. Fargo had explored each of them quickly and found no signs of anyone in them.

This canyon was a different story. Fargo's keen eyes spotted fairly recent hoofprints near the entrance.

"Somebody's been here not too long ago," he told Julia, pointing to the tracks.

"Can you tell who it was?" she asked, then realized the foolishness of that question. "No, of course you can't. I don't know what I was thinking. One set of horse tracks looks pretty much like another, doesn't it?"

Fargo grinned. "Well, not always. Sometimes you can tell quite a bit if the tracks are fresh enough. Every set of horseshoes is a little bit different. Unfortunately, these tracks are several days old, so the wind has blurred them, and even if they weren't, we don't know what the prints of your father's horse look like. We don't have anything to compare them to."

"Oh. That makes sense. Was there just one horse?"

"That's right. And it was a saddle horse, not a packhorse or a pack mule, because you can see there aren't any human footprints around, just the hoofprints."

Julia nodded. "What does that mean?"

"That the rider probably wasn't a prospector, or he would have had a pack animal with him. You saw the mules back there where Frank and Gypsum were camped. Two for riding and two for carrying supplies—and gold, if they're lucky enough to find any."

"Then who was it who rode through here?"

"No way of telling," Fargo said with a shake of his head. "One of Puma Jack's bunch, maybe."

Julia frowned. "I hope we don't run into them again."

"You and me both."

The tracks led into the canyon and didn't come out again. That meant whoever made them was still up

43

there. Fargo thought about that and went on. "Stay here while I take a look."

"But this is a bigger canyon. It looks like it runs a mile or more up into the hills."

"I reckon it does."

"I thought we would explore it together."

"I just want to scout a little first," Fargo said. "If you see anybody coming, fire a shot and I'll hightail it back here."

She nodded, looking a little nervous as she did so. Fargo didn't much blame her. With those men who had been after her back in Los Angeles possibly still on her trail, plus a gang of outlaws on the loose here in Death Valley, trouble could crop up at any time, from any direction.

He sent the Ovaro into the canyon at a fast lope, his eyes constantly scanning the rugged landscape around him. The walls of the canyon were rocky and rose at a steep slant, though not perpendicular. A man could probably climb them if he had to, but not a horse.

The mouth of the canyon was a good hundred yards wide, but the walls pinched in as Fargo rode farther into it, until the canyon was barely twenty yards from side to side. It didn't seem to have any sharp bends, but it weaved back and forth in gentle curves so that he couldn't see very far either in front of him or behind him. Julia and the wagon were out of sight.

But not out of mind. Fargo listened closely for the sound of a warning shot, hoping that he wouldn't hear one.

The dominant smell around Death Valley was the briny stench of the salt flats, but up here in the canyon the wind swirled so that it sometimes carried down odors from higher in the hills. Fargo reined in sharply as a stiff breeze blew in his face for a moment, bringing with it an unpleasant but all too familiar smell.

Something was dead up there, somewhere ahead of him in the canyon.

Fargo slid the Henry rifle from the saddle boot and levered a cartridge into the chamber. He wasn't afraid of whatever was dead, since it could no longer harm anyone. He wasn't really afraid of whoever or whatever had dealt out that death, either, but he was damn sure going to be prepared for trouble if it came.

He kneed the stallion into motion again and rode forward slowly. The canyon bent through one of its curves. The canyon floor rose slightly. The walls were higher, looming up and blocking some of the sky so that the ground ahead of Fargo was in shadow.

There was still plenty of light, though, for Fargo to be able to see the two shapes lying there in front of him, sprawled motionless in death.

4

Fargo brought the stallion to a halt and grimly studied the bodies of a man and a horse that lay on the floor of the canyon. Evidently they had been there for several days, long enough to bloat in the heat and then be torn open by the scavengers that had been at them.

It wasn't a pretty sight.

Fargo clucked to the Ovaro and walked the horse closer to the mutilated corpses. The horse had been a bay, probably a big, strong-looking animal. The man was big, too, dressed in black trousers, a white shirt, and a black vest. The shirt had a large brown stain on the front of it. Dried blood from a bullet wound, Fargo guessed.

Not much of the dead man's face was left. He'd had thick gray hair, indicating that he wasn't a youngster. He wasn't armed. There was no gun belt around his waist.

That didn't mean there hadn't been one there when he was alive. Whoever killed him could have taken his weapons. Somebody had stripped the saddle off the dead horse.

Fargo stopped the Ovaro again and studied the ground around the bodies. He saw several sets of hoofprints and boot prints. He estimated that three riders had jumped this lone man and killed him and his horse.

Then the killers had turned and ridden on up the canyon toward the Panamints. Fargo lifted his gaze toward the mountains. Maybe there was another trail through there, like the one Frank Jordan had mentioned. The trails might even connect somewhere up there.

Chances were, if Puma Jack and his gang had been using these hills around Death Valley as their hideout for the past half year, they knew most of the trails by now. Fargo wasn't going to be at all surprised if the three men who had murdered this gray-haired stranger turned out to be members of the gang.

The question that gnawed at his brain now was whether or not Julia Slauson's father had had gray hair . . .

As soon as Fargo had caught sight of the body, he had wondered if it might belong to Julia's father. He hated to think that she might have come all this way and risked as much as she had, only to find that the object of her search was already dead.

As grisly as the corpse was, he couldn't just bring her up here and have her take a look at it. He would find out first whether it was possible that the dead man could be her father.

He swung down from the saddle and walked over to the sprawled body. The man lay on his back with his arms out to the sides. Fargo couldn't tell if he had fallen that way or had been rolled over onto his back after he fell. It didn't really matter, of course; he was just as dead either way.

With his jaw clenched tightly, Fargo tried to ignore the smell and knelt beside the corpse. He searched quickly through the dead man's pockets but didn't find anything to identify him, or anything else, for that matter. The killers had robbed him and taken everything.

With the saddle and saddlebags gone, too, Fargo

had no way of knowing who the man had been. He straightened and went back to the stallion.

He dreaded the questions he was going to have to ask Julia when he got back to the wagon.

She was sitting patiently on the seat when he rode out of the canyon.

"Did you see anybody?" Fargo asked as he reined in beside the wagon.

Julia shook her head. "Not a soul. We might as well be all alone out here, Skye."

"Well, we're not," he told her.

"Oh, I know. There are probably a lot of prospectors in the hills and canyons—"

"That's not what I meant," Fargo broke in. He jerked a thumb over his shoulder. "I found somebody up the canyon."

Julia's face lit up with anticipation. "Really?"

"What color is your father's hair?" Fargo asked.

She seemed surprised by the question. "Why . . . it's white. Prematurely so. His hair turned white at a very early age. I don't remember a time when it wasn't that color."

"You don't mean gray?"

"No, I meant what I said. My father has white hair." She frowned. "What's wrong, Skye? That's an odd question to ask, about my father's hair."

"I just wanted to make sure the fella I found wasn't him."

"Well, then, why didn't you just ask hi—" She broke off her question and lifted a hand to her mouth as her eyes widened in understanding. "Oh! You mean he . . . he's . . ."

"Dead," Fargo finished for her. He nodded. "I reckon he's probably the man who left these tracks here at the canyon mouth. Somebody shot him and his horse, killed them both. Looks like it happened several days ago."

A visible shudder ran through her. "That's terrible. They must be . . . well . . ."

"They're not pretty to look at," Fargo confirmed. "The coyotes and the buzzards and the ravens have been at them."

"You don't know who the man . . . was?"

Fargo shook his head. "He didn't have anything on him to tell me. His pockets had been emptied, and his saddlebags were gone."

"What a terrible way to die."

"I don't know that there are any good ways."

"Well, what a terrible place, then. And to be left out in the open like that . . ." She shook her head.

"Drive the wagon a short distance up the canyon," Fargo told her. "You can stop and make camp for the night. I'll go back and bury the man."

"I can help you."

"No need for that," Fargo assured her.

He had started to turn away when she stopped him by saying, "Skye, you thought that man was my father, didn't you?"

"I thought he might be," Fargo answered honestly. "You hadn't given me a description of your father, so I had no way of knowing."

"I appreciate your consideration in trying to spare my feelings."

Fargo nodded and headed back up the canyon toward the spot where he had found the bodies. Digging a grave in the hard, rocky ground wasn't going to be easy, but he would manage.

He wasn't sure what he was going to do about that dead horse, though.

He wound up tying his rope to one of its hind legs and using the Ovaro to drag it over next to the canyon wall. That was the best he could do. Eventually, scavengers would finish stripping the bones, and they would be scattered throughout the canyon.

The dead man would be laid to rest properly, though. Fargo used a short shovel from his gear to scrape out a shallow grave in the hard earth. He dragged the dead man into it, covered him up, and then piled rocks on top of the mound of earth. It was difficult work in the late-afternoon heat, and Fargo was soaked in sweat by the time he was finished.

Holding his hat in his hands, Fargo said a short prayer consigning the dead man's soul to *El Señor Dios*. Then he mounted up and rode back to the wagon.

When he got there he found that Julia had built a small fire, using bits of dead brush that had blown up into the canyon from the belt of sparse vegetation between the hills and the salt flats. She had coffee on to boil, and the smell made Fargo feel a little better.

"Were you able to . . . ?" she began.

"I took care of it," he told her. "I couldn't do anything with the horse except drag it out of the middle of the canyon, but I buried the man."

"I can't help but wonder who he was, and why he was killed out here in the middle of nowhere."

Fargo got a tin cup from his saddlebags, hunkered by the fire, and used a piece of leather to protect his hand as he picked up the coffeepot and filled the cup. A sip or two of the strong black brew made him feel even better. It was amazing, he thought, how good coffee was, even when the weather was hot.

"I wouldn't be surprised if he ran into a few members of Puma Jack's gang," he said. "All his gear was gone, even his hat. They probably just shot him out of hand and robbed his corpse."

"But who *was* he?"

Her curiosity struck him as a mite strange. "We'll probably never know," he said.

"Probably not." Julia changed the subject by saying, "Do you want me to fix supper? I didn't think you'd mind if I started the coffee."

"I don't mind at all. I appreciate it. As for supper, have at it if you want, or I'll take care of it if you'd rather. I'm a pretty good trail cook. Have to be since I'm usually fending for myself."

"Why don't we work together?" she suggested with a smile.

That sounded like a good idea to Fargo, although he knew that old saying about too many cooks spoiling the broth had some truth to it. They pitched in together, frying bacon and pan bread and putting some beans on to soak. They could cook the beans in the morning and then have them for several meals afterward.

It was a pleasant, almost domestic scene, even though their surroundings were a far cry from homey. As darkness fell, the coyotes that lived in the hills began their nightly serenade.

Julia shivered at the sound and asked, "What's that? Wolves?"

Fargo shook his head. "Nope. Coyotes. Closer to dogs than wolves, but you still wouldn't want to tangle with them. Hear that yipping that sounds a little different from the others?"

Julia listened for a moment, then said, "Yes. Is that a coyote?"

"Fox," Fargo said. "You wouldn't think to look at it that there would be much wildlife in Death Valley, but it's here, you just don't see it very often. There are a lot of mountain goats up in the hills, and coyotes, foxes, and rats down here lower. Not to mention the chuckwallas."

"What in the world are those?"

"Big lizards. You want to avoid them if you see any. They're touchy, and they've got a nasty bite."

"I'll remember that. Stay away from big lizards."

"And rattlesnakes and scorpions, of course," he added.

Julia sighed in exasperation. "Is there anything out here that can't hurt you or kill you?"

Fargo thought about the outlaws and said, "Not really."

"Why would anyone want to come here, then?"

"Gold," he said simply. "Everybody wants to get rich."

"I suppose. I'd settle for finding my father and getting out of here."

After they had eaten, Fargo let the fire burn down to embers. No point in announcing their presence, even though he didn't think anybody would be looking for them. There were no hostile Indians in this area. Of course, there were the owlhoots led by Puma Jack, and there was no telling when they might come prowling around.

"I guess I'll turn in," Julia announced. "Do you plan to sleep under the wagon?"

Fargo nodded. "That's right. I'll lay my rope all the way around it to keep out any crawling varmints."

"Do we need to take turns standing guard?"

Fargo gestured at the Ovaro, who was picketed nearby. "There's the best sentry you'll find. If anybody comes around, he'll let me know."

"All right, then. Good night."

"Good night," Fargo said.

Julia climbed into the wagon and pulled the canvas flap closed behind her. Fargo shook out his bedroll under the wagon, placed the rope around the vehicle as he had told her, and then crawled into his blankets. The temperature was already dropping. It would be cold by morning.

Fargo went to sleep quickly and easily, out of long habit falling into a deep, dreamless slumber. He wasn't sure how long he had been asleep when he came instantly awake, all senses alert.

He opened his eyes and saw the Ovaro standing quietly a few yards away. Since the stallion hadn't been disturbed, Fargo was reasonably certain there were no predators around, animal or otherwise.

But if that was the case, what had awakened him?

He got the answer a moment later when Julia whispered, "Skye? Are you awake?"

Fargo sat up and said, "I am now. What's wrong?"

She was at the rear of the wagon. "Could you come up here?"

Fargo slid out of his blankets. Since there didn't seem to be any trouble, he could think of only one logical reason Julia would ask him to join her in the wagon.

He might be wrong, of course, in which case he could easily embarrass her, so he would proceed with caution until he was sure what she wanted.

He stood up, stepped onto the tailgate, and climbed into the wagon. It was pitch dark inside, but he could hear Julia's breathing.

"Are you all right?" he asked.

"I . . . I'm fine. I just thought you might like to . . . collect on part of your fee."

That was the answer Fargo expected. It was time he set her straight on that.

"Listen, Julia, you don't have to pay me that way. I know that's what you suggested back when we first talked about me looking for your father, but it's not necessary."

"I'm not sure I have enough money—"

"I'm not worried about that," Fargo assured her. "I'll help you the best I can, whether you ever pay me a penny or not."

She sounded skeptical as she said, "Why would you do that?"

"Because you need help."

For a long moment, she was silent, as if she was thinking over what he had just told her. Then she said, "So what you're saying is that you're some sort of saint?"

He felt a flash of anger. "Not hardly. Nobody's ever accused me of that."

"Then you must not find me attractive." Now she sounded hurt.

Fargo suppressed his impatience and irritation. "I find you damned attractive," he said bluntly. "I'd like nothing better than to crawl into that bunk with you right now. But I don't want it to be just because you feel like you owe me."

Now it was Julia's turn to sound angry. "You're a damned fool—you know that? I want you, Skye . . . because I want you."

Fargo grinned in the darkness. "I've been called a lot worse than a damned fool. And that was what I was waiting to hear."

He moved closer, reached out, touched warm, soft skin. Julia moaned softly. Fargo sank onto the bunk that was built along one side of the wagon and drew her into his arms. She came to him eagerly.

She wore only a thin wrapper. Fargo stripped it off of her as he kissed her, finding her lips instinctively in the darkness. He filled a hand with one of her firm, apple-sized breasts. The nipple was already hard. He stroked it with his thumb.

Julia's lips opened to his questing tongue. Fargo explored the warm, wet cavern of her mouth as he shifted his hand to her other breast and kneaded and caressed that globe of female flesh. Her hands went to the front of his buckskin trousers over the bulge formed by his hardening manhood.

Deftly, Julia worked at the buttons of his trousers until she freed his erect shaft. She wrapped her fingers around it and stroked up and down the long, thick pole. Fargo put a hand on the back of her neck, under the thick dark hair, and drove his tongue deeper into her mouth. Her tongue darted around his in a sensuous dance.

He slid his other hand down over her nude, quivering belly to her thighs, which opened instinctively to allow him to caress their inner softness. His touch moved slowly, teasingly, toward the molten core at the juncture of her legs but pulled back every time. She panted against his mouth as passion rose in her.

Finally he slid his hand onto her mound and cupped it, enjoying the feel of the thick, silky thatch of hair against his palm. His thumb nudged the tiny bud of hard flesh as his middle finger dipped lower and ran along the damp, fleshy folds of her femininity. He slipped his finger inside her wetness.

Julia's hips came up off the bunk as she thrust her pelvis against his hand, seeking to draw his finger farther into her. Her hands tightened reflexively on his shaft.

Fargo added a second finger to the first one and worked them back and forth inside her. She forgot about caressing him as she threw her arms around him and held on tightly. Her hips began to pump frenziedly as he manipulated her closer and closer to her culmination.

Finally she cried out and clutched him even harder. Her juices drenched his hand. A shudder went through her, evidently shaking her to her core. It died away slowly, and she lowered her head to rest it on his shoulder as she sagged against him.

"Oh, my," she said raggedly a few moments later, when her heavy breathing and her pounding pulse had slowed enough so that she was able to talk again. "That . . . that was wonderful, Skye." Something else occurred to her fevered brain then. "Oh! But you didn't . . . you haven't . . ."

"That's right," Fargo told her. "We're not through yet."

He lowered her onto the bunk and then quickly peeled his clothes off. When he moved into position, he found that she was ready for him, her legs spread wide to receive his shaft. He brought the tip of it to her opening and ran it up and down along the folds, wetting it thoroughly with her juices and his.

Then with a surge of his hips he penetrated her, sliding into her slowly but inexorably until his manhood was fully sheathed within her.

Julia cried out eagerly as Fargo launched into the timeless rhythm of man and woman, filling her, withdrawing, filling her again. His own arousal grew even stronger as he pounded in and out of her. The pace of their lovemaking increased as Julia, too, came closer to a climax. She raised her legs and locked her ankles together above Fargo's thrusting hips.

She met him stroke for stroke and drew his head down so that she could kiss him. This time her tongue went eagerly into his mouth. Fargo felt himself cresting and drove into her as deeply as he could, holding himself there as his climax boiled up his shaft and burst out into her in a series of throbbing white-hot explosions.

Julia screamed and clutched him with the strength that only a climaxing woman could muster. Fargo's culmination seemed to last forever as he emptied himself into her.

Finally, though, everything had to end, even something this good. As Fargo's shaft spasmed softly inside her for the last time, he started to pull out so that he could roll to the side and avoid crushing her with his weight. She held on to him, though, with her arms and legs and murmured, "No. Stay here, Skye."

Fargo obliged her, lying there for several minutes and feeling the pounding of her heart as her breasts flattened against his broad, muscular chest. He supposed she could feel his heart, too, because it was certainly pounding just like hers was.

When he sensed that she was ready for him to move, he slid off of her and lay on his side. Julia turned so that her back was to him and snuggled against him as his arms went around her. She worked the soft roundness of her hips back against his groin.

Fargo cupped her breasts, buried his face in her hair, and nuzzled her neck. She sighed in contentment as he held her. It was a quiet, tender moment they shared as they recovered from the exertions of their lovemaking.

But the position was not without its own excitements, and after only a short time, Fargo began to get hard again. Julia felt his thickening shaft prodding against her and said in pleased amazement, "Again? So soon?"

Fargo didn't bother telling her that they had all night.

He would show her instead.

By the time they fell asleep and stayed asleep, it was long after midnight, so it wasn't too surprising that they slept late the next morning. It seemed late to Fargo, anyway. The sun was almost up.

He got dressed, climbed out of the wagon, started the coffee brewing and the beans cooking in a large pot. As he sat for a moment by the fire, he thought about the previous night and grinned. Julia had proven to be as eager and inventive a lover as he had thought she would be.

"What are you smirking about?" she asked from the back of the wagon.

"I didn't know you were awake," Fargo said.

"Well, I am, and you didn't answer my question."

"Just thinking about what a pretty day it's going to be," Fargo said as he glanced up at the lightening sky. A few tendrils of pink-painted cloud showed against the pale blue.

"It won't be pretty at all, later," Julia said as she climbed out of the wagon. Instead of getting dressed, she had wrapped one of the blankets around herself. With her shoulders bare like that and her hair tousled from sleep, Fargo thought she was one of the loveliest women he had ever seen. She went on. "It'll be hot as hell."

"Can't argue with that," Fargo said.

She smiled. "Right now, though, with the air still cool and the sky looking like that, it is pretty nice."

Fargo nodded. "It sure is. Coffee?"

"That sounds *wonderful.*"

They didn't talk about what had brought them here until after they had finished breakfast. Then Fargo said, "We'll head on up the canyon this morning and take a look around."

"You're going to let me go with you?"

He took a sip of the coffee that remained in his cup. "Well, it's sort of like it was back in Blackwater. I'm worried about taking you with me, because I don't know what, if anything, we'll find up there. But I reckon I'd be more worried if I left you here alone. There's no telling when Puma Jack or some of his men might come along."

"I'm glad you're taking me, Skye. I hope we won't be separated again while we're out here."

"We'll see. Why don't you go ahead and get dressed while I tend to the mules and my horse?"

"All right." Clutching the blanket around her, she climbed up into the wagon, then paused just inside it. "Skye?"

When he looked up at her, she dropped the blanket around her feet, leaving her standing there in all her nude, glorious beauty.

"There won't be any more of that foolishness about you sleeping under the wagon, will there?"

"No," Fargo said with a shake of his head. "I reckon not."

*   *   *

Fargo kept them on the opposite side of the canyon as they passed the spot where the dead horse lay, but he couldn't get them far enough away so that Julia couldn't see and smell the corpse. She saw the mound of rocks that marked the dead man's grave as well, and she was solemn as she handled the reins and kept the mule team moving.

"I'd still like to know who that man was and why he was killed," she said.

"We can ask around when we get back to Blackwater," Fargo said. "Somebody might recognize the description."

He didn't add that because of the damage scavengers had done to the body, all he could describe was the dead man's size, clothes, and hair color.

He was glad when they were out of sight of that place of death. They followed the canyon on into the hills, where it ran for more than a mile. Gradually, the floor of the canyon rose until they came out on a flat, level shoulder that jutted out from the side of the hill. Fargo reined in and looked around.

The terracelike ledge they were on stretched as far as he could see to the north and south. It was wide enough for several men to ride abreast. He had been right in his guess that many of the canyons connected to a single trail.

"What is this?" Julia asked.

"I've heard it said that at one time, this whole valley was nothing but a big lake, back in the days when there weren't any people around here except maybe a few Indians. I reckon if that's true, this ledge could be the shoreline of that old lake."

"As dry as it is now, it's hard to believe there was ever that much water here."

Fargo nodded. "I know what you mean. But if you go out there on the salt flats and dig down a couple of feet, you'll find all the water you'd ever want. The only problem is that it's even saltier than the ocean."

"I didn't see any sign of my father in that canyon, or of anyone else, for that matter."

Fargo had noticed a few tracks, some shiny spots here and there on the rocks where horseshoes had nicked them, but other than that he agreed with Julia. He thought the tracks he had seen had been left by the men who killed that gray-haired stranger.

"The ledge is wide enough for the wagon," he said. "We'll travel up here for a while. That'll give us a good vantage point."

They were at least five hundred feet higher in elevation than the salt flats, which were below sea level. That old lake, if indeed there had been such a thing, had been a deep one.

As they moved along the ledge, Fargo looked down over stark, sweeping vistas. From up here he could see the fan-shaped hills, the canyons and washes, the distant salt flats that now shone brilliantly white in the sun.

As they headed farther south, a surprising bit of color caught Fargo's eye. It was only a drab green, but even that was rare in this land of grays and browns and tans. As they came closer, he saw a few small bushes growing around a cluster of rocks and knew that within those rocks there had to be a spring.

He rode ahead to check it out and found that he was right. A spring bubbled out from a cleft in the hillside and trickled down to form a small pool in the rocks. The pool was only about four feet across, but the water was clear and inviting.

Fargo swung down from the saddle and knelt beside the pool, holding the Ovaro back while he scooped up a handful of water and smelled it. It had a slight mineral odor, but not bad. Fargo put out his tongue and tasted. Finding the water cool and good, he drank what was cupped in his hand and reached down for more.

Satisfied that the water was all right, he moved aside and let the stallion drink, too. Then he stood up and took off his hat to wave Julia on. She brought the wagon to a stop beside the clump of rocks that formed the pool.

"This is one of those springs Mr. Jordan talked about, isn't it?" she asked.

Fargo nodded as he put his hat back on. "That's right. There are several of them on this side of the valley, along the Panamints. They're more plentiful on the other side, but the water's not quite as good. This is all snowmelt, and it hasn't had a chance to get much salt in it yet."

Julia climbed down from the wagon and asked, "I don't suppose the spring is big enough so that I could have a bath?"

"I'm afraid not," Fargo said, shaking his head a little regretfully. The thought of Julia rising nude and wet from a pond of clean, clear water was a mighty appealing one. "You can probably wash up a mite, though, if the mules don't drink it dry first."

She made a face. "I suppose the animals have first call on the water. We need them more than we need to be clean."

Actually, Fargo filled all the canteens first, then let the mules at the pool. Not wanting them to founder, he didn't allow them to drink their fill but instead tugged them away after a short time. He would let them drink again later.

Since it was past midday, they ate a cold lunch of leftover bacon, beans, and biscuits. As Julia sat on one of the rocks next to the spring, she said, "It's almost nice here. In a way, I hate to leave."

"We can't find your father by staying here," Fargo pointed out.

"I know," she said with a sigh. "The water just makes it seem cooler somehow . . ."

She might have said more, but at that instant, the sharp crack of a rifle filled the air, and Julia screamed as a bullet spanged off the rock next to her hand.

5

Fargo's instincts took over, galvanizing his muscles into action and flinging him across the shallow pool toward Julia. He tackled her, bringing her to the ground among the rocks. She cried out in pain as she landed hard.

Better a bruise than a bullet hole, though. Another slug ricocheted near them. Fargo said, "Get as low as you can and stay there!"

Then he sprang up and sprinted toward the Ovaro, who stood steadfast despite the shooting. Fargo heard the wind-rip of another bullet close by his head as he snagged the Henry from the saddle boot. He dived behind another of the small boulders.

He didn't know yet where the shots were coming from, or even how many riflemen were shooting at them. Until he knew that, he couldn't fight back, so he risked lifting his head long enough to take a look around.

A hundred yards to the south, the ledge that marked the shoreline of the ancient lake twisted around some rocks. Fargo saw a puff of smoke from among those rocks just as another rifle shot blasted out. The slug whined overhead.

So far, Fargo thought he had heard only one gun, and what he saw seemed to confirm that. Gun smoke drifted up only from that one spot among the distant rocks. It was a good bet there was only one bush-whacker.

Knowing that didn't tell Fargo who the rifleman was or why he was trying to kill them, but at least now he knew they were dealing with just one enemy.

Fargo waited until the bushwhacker's rifle had cracked again, having noticed that the man's shots were spaced out a little. That might mean the man was using a single-shot rifle and had to reload after each round. He hoped he was right as he surged up on his knees and fired three times as fast as he could work the repeater's lever.

Then he hit the dirt again and waited to see what would happen.

Nothing did. The bushwhacker's rifle had fallen silent. Did that mean he was hit, or was he just trying to lure Fargo into the open again?

"Skye?" Julia called. "Skye, are you all right?"

"I'm fine," he told her. "How about you?"

"Just scared. Who's shooting at us?"

"Your guess is as good as mine. Could be one of Puma Jack's men. They seem like a pretty proddy bunch. Maybe even Jack himself."

"But why?"

"Pure meanness, maybe. They might not need a reason."

Still, no more shots came from the rocks where the unknown rifleman had been hidden. Suddenly, Fargo heard a loud, raucous sound. It was the unmistakable bray of a donkey.

He knew a lot of the prospectors who came to Death Valley used donkeys as pack animals instead of mules or horses. These burros, as the Mexicans called them, were small but strong and were almost as surefooted as mountain goats.

It seemed highly unlikely to Fargo that an outlaw would be riding a donkey. Stranger things had happened, he supposed, but the braying made Fargo wonder if the man trying to kill them was a prospector. Maybe the man had mistaken them for someone else . . .

"Hey!" he yelled into the silence. "Hold your fire! I think there's been a misunderstanding here!"

A scratchy, querulous voice came back at him, raised so that its owner could be heard. "Ain't no misunderstandin'!" the hidden gunman shouted. "Just a mistake, and you made it by ridin' in range o' my rifle, you no-good owlhoot!"

Movement seen from the corner of his eye caught Fargo's attention, and he glanced around to see that Julia had crawled around in the rocks so that she could see him. She gave him a confused frown and shook her head. Fargo took that to mean that she didn't recognize the voice.

Neither did he. As far as he knew, he had never heard it before.

"We're not outlaws!" he shouted. "We thought you were one of Puma Jack's gang!"

That brought a burst of profanity so scorching it seemed to turn the very air blue. The rifleman concluded by saying, "I'd apologize for talkin' like that around a lady, but there ain't no lady here, only that harlot!"

"Skye!" Julia hissed. "He's got no right to call me that, no matter who he is!"

Fargo was a little more concerned that the bushwhacker might shoot them instead of just calling them names. He motioned for her to be quiet while he thought about what he ought to do next.

"All right!" he shouted. "We did make a mistake! You're not one of Puma Jack's men! But we're not outlaws, either! You've got us mixed up with somebody else!"

"Prove it!"

"My name is Skye Fargo! The lady with me is Miss Julia Slauson! We're out here looking for her father!"

Fargo's voice was getting a little hoarse from all the yelling. But nobody was shooting at anybody now, at least for the moment. That was an improvement.

A couple of minutes of silence went by, and Fargo wondered if the rifleman had slipped back around the bend and left. But then the man called, "Come on out where I can get a gander at you!"

"So you can ventilate us? I don't think so."

"I'll step out, too, so's you'll have just as good a chance at me. Sound fair to you?"

Fargo thought it over for a second and called, "On three?"

"Sure! Count it off!"

Fargo glanced at Julia. "Stay down and out of sight," he told her.

"Shouldn't I show him that I'm not dangerous, too?" she asked.

"No, just stay put. We'll see what happens." Fargo turned his head back toward the hidden rifleman and shouted, "One . . . two . . . *three!*"

He stood up and stepped into plain sight on the trail. He halfway expected the bushwhacker to start shooting again, so he was ready to leap for cover and return that fire if he had to.

Instead of being treacherous, though, the man followed Fargo's example and moved out from the rocks where he had been hidden. Though Fargo couldn't make out all the details at this distance, he saw that the man was an old-timer, with a white beard and a battered hat with the brim pushed up in the front. The rifle in his hands was an ancient single-shot weapon, just as Fargo had suspected.

"Where's the gal?" the man shouted.

"I told her to stay down," Fargo answered honestly. "I wasn't sure how tricky you might be!"

65

Even at this distance, Fargo heard the man's disgusted snort. "Ain't nobody ever said that Chuckwalla Smith ain't a man of his word! I ought'a shoot you for just implyin' such slander!"

Fargo had never heard of Chuckwalla Smith, but the nickname indicated that the man had been around Death Valley for quite some time, and his rough garb marked him as a prospector.

"I'm going to put my rifle down," Fargo said. "Why don't you come on in and we'll talk things over?"

"I ain't puttin' my gun down!"

"I'm not asking you to," Fargo said. He held the Henry out at arm's length, then bent and placed it carefully on the ground. He stepped back away from the rifle.

Chuckwalla Smith hesitated, then moved forward slowly.

"Is he coming?" Julia asked, quietly enough so that the old prospector couldn't hear her.

"He's coming," Fargo answered from the side of his mouth. He really wasn't taking that big a chance by putting his rifle down. He still had the Colt on his hip, and Chuckwalla was already within range of the handgun. If he made a threatening move, Fargo would draw the revolver and defend himself.

Chuckwalla kept the rifle slanted across his chest, though, and didn't point it toward Fargo. He stopped about twenty feet away and said, "I'd feel a heap better if'n that gal would step out where I can see her, so I'd know she ain't drawin' a bead on me."

Fargo motioned with his left hand but didn't take his eyes off Chuckwalla. "Come on out, Julia."

She stood up and moved out from behind the rocks. Fargo saw the old-timer's gaze flick toward her. Chuckwalla's eyes brightened in appreciation of what he saw.

"I got to admit, ma'am, you're a heap prettier than

the gal I thought you was. And you, mister, now that I get a better look at you, I don't recollect seein' you with Puma Jack's bunch before."

"That's because I don't ride with Puma Jack," Fargo said. "I never even heard of the man until yesterday."

"You said your name is Skye Fargo?"

"That's right."

"I've heard tell of a fella named Fargo. Some folks call him the Trailsman."

"That's me," Fargo confirmed.

"Well, I've never heard it said that the Trailsman was a owlhoot, so I reckon you're tellin' the truth. Sorry I blazed away at you."

An apology was one thing, but Chuckwalla's first shot had come awfully close to hitting Julia. Fargo was still angry about that.

"Next time be sure who you're shooting at," he snapped.

Chuckwalla's eyes narrowed. "Listen, mister, if you'd been dodgin' killers like I have, you'd likely be a mite quick on the trigger, too."

"Puma Jack's gang has been after you?"

The old-timer nodded. "That's right. From what I've heard and seen, he's tryin' to wipe out all the prospectors on this side o' Death Valley."

Fargo frowned. "What do you mean by that?"

"I started up from the Owlsheads about a week ago. Figured I'd head for Blackwater to pick up some supplies. So far I've come across three camps where the fellas has been murdered and the camps tore up. Johnny Bear, Humpback Al, and Jonesey are all dead." Chuckwalla's voice broke a little. "Shot down like dogs, ever' blessed one of 'em."

"They were friends of yours?" Fargo asked.

"Damn right they were. Sure, we're all rivals, I reckon you could say, but they was good fellas anyway." Chuckwalla finally let his rifle drop to his side,

67

holding it in his left hand. With his right he scratched at his tangled beard. "Those owlhoots jumped some o' the other boys, but they got away and are hidin' up in the hills. They had to abandon their camps."

"And the outlaws tried to kill you, too?"

Chuckwalla jerked his head in a nod. "Yep, they've taken potshots at me a couple o' times. But I didn't try to fight 'em. I just kept movin' and give 'em the slip each time."

"But you tried to bushwhack us," Fargo pointed out.

The old prospector sighed. "Yeah, I should'a just laid low when I spotted you, but I seen there was just two of you, and I reckon I wasn't thinkin' straight on account o' my friends bein' killed. I ain't a bushwhacker by nature, Fargo, and I don't mind sayin' I'm a mite ashamed of what I done. Especially considerin' the fact you got a innocent woman with you."

That brought up another question in Fargo's mind. "You mentioned there's a woman with the outlaws?"

"Yep," Chuckwalla replied with a nod. "Most o' the time she wears pants and rides astride like a man, but sometimes she puts on a dress. Got hair black as midnight. I see now that yours ain't quite that dark, ma'am. I'm sorry."

Julia brushed some of the brunette strands back from her face. "That's all right, Mr. Smith," she told him. "It was an honest mistake."

She was a little quicker to forgive than he was, Fargo thought, and yet it was obvious that Chuckwalla Smith had been genuinely mistaken about their identities. And what the old pelican had told them was certainly interesting.

"You say you're out here lookin' for your pa?" Chuckwalla went on, addressing the question to Julia.

She nodded. "That's right. His name is Arthur Slauson. Do you know him?"

"Can't say as I do," Chuckwalla replied with a shake of his head. "Might know him by another name, though. What's he look like?"

"He's forty-six years old, and he has white hair. About as tall as Mr. Fargo here, but not as broad-shouldered. And his eyebrows are rather bushy."

Fargo thought he saw a flicker of something in Chuckwalla's eyes, but the old prospector shook his head again and said, "Don't recollect ever seein' somebody who looks like that out here in Death Valley. How long's he been missin'?"

"He came here approximately six months ago, and I haven't heard from him since."

"Sorry I can't help you, ma'am," Chuckwalla said curtly.

Fargo wondered if the old man knew more than he was telling them. It was possible Julia's father had been one of the murdered prospectors Chuckwalla had mentioned by their nicknames. Maybe he didn't want to tell her that because he didn't want to hurt her, but if that was the case he wasn't really sparing her by withholding the truth.

Fargo thought it might be better to hash that out with Chuckwalla later, out of Julia's hearing. The old-timer might be more forthcoming then.

For now, Fargo said, "What you've told us sort of ties in with what we've already discovered. Yesterday Puma Jack's gang attacked a couple of prospectors in a canyon north of here."

"Not Frank and Gypsum!" Chuckwalla exclaimed.

Fargo nodded. "That's right. Don't worry, though; neither of them was killed. Frank was wounded, but it shouldn't be too bad. Gypsum came through without a scratch."

"I'm plumb glad to hear that," Chuckwalla said fervently. "They're good old boys, those two."

"But we did find a dead man in another canyon between here and there," Fargo went on. "He'd been shot and left for the coyotes and the buzzards. His horse was killed, too."

"Any sign o' who done it?"

"Three riders, from the looks of it. That's all I could tell."

Chuckwalla spat on the stony ground. "Three o' Jack's men, sure as shootin'. What did this fella look like?"

"He was middle-aged," Fargo said, basing that guess on the gray hair. "Sort of beefy. He was wearing black trousers and vest and a white shirt."

"Don't know him. That don't sound like anybody I've ever seen around these parts. Lots of folks come to Death Valley, though." Chuckwalla spat again. "It's just that these days, most of 'em never leave."

Since some of the food left from lunch was still sitting out, Fargo invited Chuckwalla to join them. Evidently the old man had been around here for quite a while and was very familiar with the desolate landscape. Now that they weren't shooting at each other anymore, Fargo thought it might be useful to talk more with him.

Chuckwalla sat down on a rock next to the little pool and tore hungrily into the plate of biscuits and beans Julia gave him. "Like I said, I was headin' for Blackwater to buy supplies," he said between bites. "I been runnin' low on rations for quite a while, but I didn't want to leave my claim."

"Find some color?" Fargo asked.

Chuckwalla's head bobbed up and down as he chewed. He swallowed and said, "Not what I'd call a big strike, mind you, but good enough I was a-feared somebody would jump it if I left. Finally got to where I had to, though, or else wind up starvin' to death. Prob'ly a good thing I lit out when I did, or that gang o' varmints might'a jumped me whilst I was in camp and killed me."

"What are you going to do now?" Julia asked.

"Go on to Blackwater, get my supplies, and head back, o' course," Chuckwalla replied.

"You're not worried about Puma Jack's bunch?"

"Well, dagnab it, o' course I'm worried! Like I done told you, they're tryin' to murder ever' prospector on this side o' Death Valley! But I been trampin' around this hellhole for nigh on to ten years without ever findin' a claim as good as the one I got now. I'll be damned if I'm gonna let anybody run me off it."

Fargo wasn't surprised by the crusty old-timer's attitude. He had known plenty of prospectors and miners, and all of them felt the same way when it came to gold and silver and the other precious metals that lured them on. They would defy all odds for a chance to strike it rich, even when a murderous outlaw gang was on the prod.

"How about you folks?" Chuckwalla went on. "Now that you know about Puma Jack's rampage, you gonna light a shuck back to the settlement?"

Fargo looked at Julia. It was her father that was missing, after all. The decision would have to be up to her.

"I . . . I can't turn back," she said after a moment. "I know it's dangerous for us to be out here, but I have to find my father."

Chuckwalla glanced slyly at Fargo. "You go along with that, mister?"

"I told Miss Slauson I'd help her," Fargo said. "Man of my word, remember?"

The old-timer grunted and went back to cleaning his plate. When he was finished, he stood up and said, "I got to go get Lilac."

"Lilac?" Fargo repeated.

"My burro. Call her that on account of she's mighty fond o' the smell o' lilac water. She sniffed some once whilst we was in a settlement and like to went plumb crazy over it."

"How sweet," Julia said. "You should get her some."

Chuckwalla eyed her and said, "She's a burro, ma'am, not a woman. I been out here in the desert a durned long time, but I still know the diff'rence."

"Of course," Julia said, and Fargo saw to his amusement that she was blushing a little. He looked down to hide his grin.

"I'll walk over there with you," he said to Chuckwalla. He still wanted to talk to the old-timer where Julia couldn't hear.

"It's a free country," Chuckwalla said with a shrug.

Julia began cleaning up after the meal while the two men walked along the trail toward the rocks where Chuckwalla had hidden earlier. Fargo didn't like leaving her there alone, but he didn't plan to go very far.

He didn't waste any time getting down to business. "When Julia described her father to you, I thought for a second you looked like what she was saying meant something to you."

Chuckwalla glanced sharply at him. "What? Naw, I don't know what you're talkin' about, Fargo. I . . . I never heard o' the fella, nor seen anybody who looks like that."

"I think you're lying," Fargo said bluntly. "Was one of the murdered prospectors you found really Arthur Slauson?"

"What makes you think that?"

"I told you, the way you reacted when Julia was describing him to you."

Chuckwalla ran his fingers through his tangled beard. "Hell, no, he weren't one o' them poor boys that got theirselves shot. Johnny Bear was as big as a bear—that's how he got his name. Humpback Al . . . well, I reckon you can guess about him. And Jonesey was a scrawny little cuss, and bald as an egg, to boot. Not a one of 'em looked anything like what the gal was sayin', and I ain't seen no other prospectors 'round here who do, neither."

Fargo heard sincerity in the old man's voice and was convinced that Chuckwalla was telling the truth—at least as far as it went.

"What about somebody besides a prospector?"

Chuckwalla snorted. "Ain't nobody else out here."

"What about those outlaws?"

Chuckwalla stared at Fargo. "Are you askin' me if the gal's pa belongs to Puma Jack's gang?"

"I don't reckon it's very likely," Fargo said, "but I like to consider all the possibilities."

"Well, I can't help you there. I ain't never seen any o' them bandits close up. Ever' time our trails crossed, I skedaddled away from there as fast as I could."

Fargo nodded. He had reached a dead end. He still sensed that Chuckwalla knew more than he was saying, but the old pelican just wasn't about to admit it.

They rounded the bend in the trail, and Fargo saw a long-eared, shaggy-maned burro staked out not far away. The creature let out a bray of greeting as it spotted its master.

Chuckwalla laughed and rubbed a tousled clump of hair between the burro's ears. "I done told you I'd come back for you, Lilac," he said. "When are you gonna learn to believe me?"

The burro bared its teeth and brayed again.

Chuckwalla pulled up the picket stake and led the burro by the reins. He came over to Fargo and said, "Lilac, this here is Mr. Skye Fargo. That's right, the one they call the Trailsman. He's a famous fella. Fargo, meet Lilac."

Fargo felt vaguely ridiculous being introduced to a donkey, but he rubbed between Lilac's ears as Chuckwalla had done.

"Hello, Lilac," he said.

The burro tried to bite him. Fargo snatched his hand back just in time to avoid the big, blunt teeth.

The old prospector chuckled. "I plumb forgot to tell you . . . Lilac don't cotton much to strangers. I reckon you could say she's a one-man donkey."

"You're welcome to her," Fargo muttered.

With Chuckwalla leading the burro, they went back to the wagon. The mules had drunk the little pool almost dry, but it was slowly refilling as more water trickled out of the spring.

"I'll be seein' you folks," Chuckwalla said as Fargo swung up onto the Ovaro's back and Julia climbed to the wagon seat and took up the reins. "Be careful. Death Valley ain't no place for greenhorns, even in the best o' circumstances, and with them outlaws marauding around, I reckon it's even worse."

"We'll keep our eyes open," Fargo promised. "Don't go taking any more potshots at people when you don't know who they are."

"Now, I already said I was sorry about that," Chuckwalla grumbled. "Ain't no need to keep proddin' me about it."

With a grin, Fargo lifted a hand in farewell and then wheeled the stallion around and headed south. Julia got the wagon rolling behind him. When Fargo glanced back, he saw Chuckwalla plodding north toward Blackwater, leading the burro behind him.

Fargo hoped the old-timer made it safely to the settlement. Despite Chuckwalla's crotchety nature and tendency to being trigger-happy, Fargo liked him.

He just hoped that Chuckwalla had been telling the truth and wasn't hiding anything. Fargo still wasn't completely convinced of that.

They followed the ledge that marked the shoreline of the ancient lake until it petered out at the head of the next canyon, which was a long, narrow defile between high gravelly hills. There was another spring here, and the water was just as good as what came from the other one. It didn't form a pool here, however, but instead ran down a slope until the trickle disappeared in a stretch of sand. They could top off their canteens but would have to fill them directly at the spring.

"We'll stop here tonight," Fargo said. "Then in the morning we'll go back out through this canyon."

As they were making camp, Julia said, "Skye, do you really think we'll ever find my father?"

"If I didn't think there was a good chance of it, I never would have come out here," Fargo said. "Death Valley is a big place, but not so big that we can't cover all of it."

"Chuckwalla said he'd been here for ten years."

"Prospecting is a lot different than looking for a person. It takes a lot more time. Don't give up hope, Julia. We've barely gotten started."

She sighed. "I just thought . . . I hoped . . . we would run into someone by now who knew him and could tell us where to look for him. And now we have to worry about those outlaws, too. Why do you think they're trying to kill all the prospectors?"

"I reckon they must want Death Valley as their own private hiding place, where they can come back between jobs and not have to worry about anybody coming after them."

"They don't have to kill everyone in order to do that," Julia said. "The prospectors wouldn't bother them."

"Prospectors might tell the law where to look for them, though, if a posse came up here. With nobody to pay attention to their comings and goings, they have to worry less about someone tracking them down."

She nodded. "I guess you're right. Killing everyone just seems like an awfully drastic solution."

"Owlhoots aren't usually known for their kindness," Fargo said.

They built a small fire that gave off little smoke

and cooked their supper before nightfall. By the time darkness settled down over the rugged landscape, Fargo had already extinguished the flames. Now that he knew about Puma Jack's quest to wipe out everyone else in Death Valley, it was more important than ever that he and Julia not draw attention to themselves.

They sat on the lowered tailgate of the wagon and watched the stars come out, kindling into existence against the darkening sky.

"It's beautiful," Julia said. She rested her head against Fargo's shoulder, and he just naturally slipped an arm around her.

"Lonesome, though," he said as a coyote began to howl in the distance.

"And scary. Just knowing that those bloodthirsty outlaws are out there somewhere . . ." He felt a little shudder go through her.

His arm tightened around her. "Don't worry about them. We'll stay out of their way and maybe they'll stay out of ours."

What Fargo had learned from Chuckwalla Smith bothered him more than he was letting on. If not for having Julia with him, he might have been tempted to go after the murderous Puma Jack and his gang. Fargo never had cottoned much to cold-blooded killers.

Right now, though, he had to look after Julia, try to find her father, and then see that she got back safely to civilization. That was a tall enough order for one man, even the Trailsman.

As they sat there together, she rested her hand on his thigh. After a few minutes her fingers began to slide toward his groin. Fargo didn't try to stop her as she started caressing his manhood through the buckskin trousers. He grew hard under her skillful touch.

"I want to do something for you," she whispered

as she began unfastening the buttons on the trousers. "You just sit there and enjoy yourself."

She freed his shaft from the buckskins and stroked up and down the thick pole. The soft touch of her hands made him swell even more until the shaft was jutting up tall and proud from his groin.

Then she bent over and pressed her lips to the head. Fargo bit back the groan of pleasure that tried to well up his throat.

Julia's tongue came out, and the tip of it darted and flickered around the crown of his manhood. She slid a hand down into his trousers to cup the heavy sacks at the base of the shaft. As she caressed them, she began to lick the head of it, hotly gliding her tongue around and around.

Fargo suppressed the urge to thrust his member deep into her mouth and down her very throat. He let her set the pace. She continued licking up and down until she had laved the entire shaft. It was exquisite torment for Fargo to hold back.

Finally, after long, tantalizing minutes, Julia raised her head slightly, opened her mouth, and took him inside it. Her lips closed around the tip of his manhood and she sucked gently as she stroked lower down. Gradually, she swallowed more and more of him until he filled her entire mouth. He rested a hand on the back of her bobbing head as she continued to drive him mad with pleasure.

Skye Fargo was nothing if not human, and there was only so much of that he could stand. He felt his juices rising and knew that it wouldn't be much longer until culmination washed over him.

"Be careful," he whispered to Julia.

With a toss of her hair, she lifted her head from him just long enough to gasp, "Go ahead, Skye! Give it to me!" Then her hungry mouth closed around his shaft again and she sucked even harder.

Fargo couldn't hold back now. His hands dug into

her shoulders as his hips rose from the tailgate. His climax thundered through the both of them, the muscles in her throat working to take everything he had to give her.

When the spasms were finally over, Julia milked the last of his essence from him. Breathing heavily from her own excitement, she lay sprawled across his lap, resting her head on his thigh. Fargo stroked the dark hair that fanned out around her head.

Both of them caught their breath, and then Fargo lifted her until she was sitting beside him again. She snuggled against him.

"Did you enjoy that?" she asked.

"You know I did. Just like you're going to enjoy what I'm about to do for you."

"Why, Mr. Fargo!" she said with a little laugh. "Whatever do you mean?"

Fargo pulled her over backward into the wagon and showed her.

More than once, in fact.

6

Fargo woke up to the crackling of flames. His instincts telling him that something was wrong, he was instantly alert and reached for his Colt as he surged up off the bunk inside the wagon.

He and Julia had spent a very pleasant night making love to each other and then sleeping snuggled together in the narrow bunk.

Julia was gone now, though, and Fargo was afraid something had happened to her. The Ovaro should have awakened him if any strangers came around, but maybe something had happened to the big stallion.

That thought, and his concern about Julia, made him leap to the tailgate and vault out of the wagon, gun in hand.

Julia looked up in surprise from where she knelt beside the big campfire she had built. "Skye!" she exclaimed. "What's wrong?"

Fargo's gaze flicked around the camp, making certain there was no imminent threat. The fire's glare spread out in a large circle but revealed no enemies. A glance at the sky with its line of gray to the east told Fargo the time was about an hour before dawn.

With a curse, he jammed his Colt back in its holster and reached for a nearby water bucket. Julia cried out in surprise and a little anger as Fargo dashed the water onto the fire, extinguishing the flames.

"Why did you do that?" she demanded. "I was about to put the coffee on and start breakfast!"

"A fire that size can be seen for twenty miles out here," Fargo snapped. "You've just told anybody who cares to look where we are."

Julia turned her head toward the smoking, smoldering embers. "But . . . but I didn't think . . . I didn't mean to . . . Oh, my God, Skye!"

She stood up and came toward him. He put his arms around her and patted her on the back. He wasn't going to tell her that everything was all right, because it might not be. But he wasn't going to scold her any more, either.

"I just . . . I woke up and couldn't go back to sleep, so I thought it would be smart if I got breakfast ready. I thought we could get an earlier start on the day that way."

"That would be fine if not for the fact that we've got those outlaws to worry about," Fargo told her. "We'll get everything else ready to go, then wait until the sun's up to build another fire and fix breakfast."

She nodded. "I'm really sorry. I just didn't think."

Fargo didn't say anything. He reached back into the wagon to get his shirt and then pulled it over his head.

When he had his boots and hat on, he tended to the animals, making sure the stallion and the mules had some grain from the supplies in the wagon. There wasn't enough graze in Death Valley to keep them alive, although the mountain goats managed somehow.

By the time he had the team hitched up and the Ovaro saddled, the eastern sky was a bright reddish-orange. A few minutes later, the sun peeked over the Black Mountains on the other side of the valley and cast its glow across the landscape.

"Now we can build a fire," Fargo said.

Julia was still apologetic. Fargo told her to forget it. What was done was done, and there was no point in dwelling on it.

After they had eaten and refilled their canteens and water barrel, they started down the canyon toward the band of rocky, brush-dotted ground between the hills and the salt flats. This canyon ran straight for a couple of miles. It was late morning when they emerged from it.

They hadn't seen any signs of other human beings, either prospectors or outlaws.

Fargo led the way south again. It was quite a distance to the next main canyon they would need to explore, and by late in the day they still hadn't reached it. They had passed some smaller canyons and washes, and as he had done before, Fargo rode up them quickly, had a look around, and didn't see anyone.

In one wash, though, he found what was left of a campsite, and nearby was a mound of dirt and rocks marking a grave. That had to be the resting place of one of the murdered prospectors Chuckwalla had told them about, he thought.

He didn't say anything about that discovery to Julia. She was already worried enough about her father.

While the sun was still a short distance above the Panamints, Fargo called a halt. They stopped in front of an open, covelike space that looked almost like something had taken a bite out of the hillside that sloped down toward them.

"That'll make a good place to camp," Fargo said. "We won't have to worry so much about a fire being seen in there."

"Skye, I'm still sorry about that," Julia said.

Fargo waved it off. "Don't worry about it now."

They had seen no one during the day, and it was possible nobody had noticed the fire Julia had built early that morning.

They would know more about that after tonight, Fargo thought.

He didn't know if the outlaws were aware of their presence in Death Valley or not. He had pitched in to help Frank Jordan and Gypsum Dailey when they were under attack by some of Puma Jack's men, but the owlhoots had never gotten a good look at him before they fled. It was possible the gang still didn't know that he and Julia were here.

If the outlaws had come to regard Death Valley as their own private hideout, though, sooner or later they would notice a pair of newcomers. Fargo figured it was only a matter of time. His hope was that they could find Arthur Slauson and get out of there before Puma Jack came after them.

He built a fire and kept it small even though it was fairly well-concealed by the gravelly walls that rose around them. The coffee was brewing and the bacon was frying by the time the sun went down.

They ate and drank and then put out the fire. The nighttime chill drove them into the wagon. As soon as they were inside, Julia was in his arms, kissing and caressing him. He thought she made love with a little extra passion on this night. He didn't know if she did that because she still felt guilty about starting the blaze that morning and was trying to make it up to him, or if her natural passion was just that strong.

Either way, he enjoyed himself immensely and then drifted off to sleep with her in his arms.

For the second night in a row, Fargo came awake with a premonition of disaster. This time, though, Julia was still lying next to him, sound asleep.

The Ovaro was picketed close to the wagon. Fargo

heard the big black-and-white stallion blow loudly through his nose and shift around. The horse sensed trouble, and Fargo knew the Ovaro's reaction was what had roused him from sleep.

He sat up and reached for his gun. Beside him, Julia stirred and started to mutter a sleepy question. Fargo's free hand covered her mouth.

That startled her fully awake. Before she could start to struggle, he leaned close to her and hissed into her ear, "It's me! Don't move, and don't say anything. Something's wrong."

For a second she just lay there, her sleep-drugged brain evidently struggling to comprehend what he had said, but then she nodded in understanding. He took his hand away from her mouth.

"Stay here," he whispered. "Something's spooked my horse. I'm going to take a look around."

One of her hands found his arm in the darkness and clutched it. "Skye, no!" she whispered as quietly as he had. "Don't go out there!"

"You'll be all right," Fargo assured her. "Keep your pistol in your hand, and if anybody but me tries to climb in here, shoot them."

She held on to him for a second, then let go. "Let me know it's you when you come back. I'd hate to shoot you."

"I wouldn't care for it myself," Fargo told her dryly. He moved to the rear of the wagon, silently swung a leg over the tailgate, and let himself down to the ground.

In the moonlight, he saw the Ovaro standing about ten feet away, head up, ears pricked, muscles tensed for action. The stallion was looking out toward the salt flats.

Fargo looked in the same direction and didn't see anything moving, but he trusted the Ovaro's senses at least as much as he trusted his own. If the horse thought there was danger out there, Fargo believed it, too. Dropping into a crouch, he moved toward the front of the little cul-de-sac where they had made camp.

The Ovaro's head swung suddenly to the side, and if that wasn't enough of a warning, Fargo heard gravel rattle behind him, too. He twisted around and brought up the Colt, but before he could fire, a dark, looming shape came hurtling out of the darkness and crashed into him.

The collision knocked Fargo backward. As he fell, the thought flashed through his mind that someone had jumped on him from up above on the hillside. The heavy weight bore him down and smashed him to the ground, stunning him and knocking the breath out of his lungs.

He managed to hang on to the revolver, though, and instinct sent it slashing at his attacker. The barrel thudded against something hard, and Fargo heard a grunt in the darkness. He hoped he had bashed in the son of a bitch's skull.

No such luck. The man stayed on top of him, grappling with him and trying to get his hands around Fargo's throat. Fargo arched his back, throwing his opponent off-balance, and struck again with the gun. This time the man sagged and fell to the side.

Fargo rolled over and came up onto his knees. Feet rushed at him. The man who had jumped him hadn't been alone.

Fargo still had the gun in his hand, but he hesitated to fire. Chances were, these assailants were some of Puma Jack's gang, but it was possible they were prospectors who thought *he* was an outlaw, just like Chuckwalla Smith had at first. Fargo didn't want to ventilate an innocent man.

Instead he launched himself forward in a tackle, guided by the sound of charging footsteps. He crashed into someone in the dark, and both men went down.

Fargo was on top this time, however, and his left fist smashed into the man's face. The man's head bounced hard on the stony ground. He went limp.

That made two of them, Fargo thought. How many more were there?

He found out a second later as someone grabbed him from behind. A gun barrel smashed across his wrist, forcing him to drop the Colt.

"We'll hang on to this wild bronc," a harsh voice grated in his ear. "You boys see if you can tame him."

Fargo's eyes were well-adjusted to the darkness. He saw two men coming at him from the front. Two more men held him, one on each arm. Fargo figured the two in front would take turns slugging him into unconsciousness, maybe even death. Fighting back wasn't going to make anything worse than it already was.

He threw his weight against the men holding him and jerked both feet off the ground as the other two closed in. With the superb athleticism that an active life had given him, he drew his legs back and snapped them forward again in a powerful kick. His heels smashed into the chests of the men in front of him and sent them flying backward. The impact made the two men holding him stagger back the other direction.

One of them fell, and that dragged Fargo and the other man down, too. Fargo jerked his right arm free and brought the elbow up and back as hard and fast as he could. The blow connected solidly with a man's jaw. That left just one man holding Fargo.

The Trailsman rolled over, taking that startled individual with him. The man wound up with Fargo on top of him. With his free hand, Fargo slashed a side-handed blow across the man's throat. The clutching fingers fell away.

Taking on half a dozen men in a hand-to-hand

brawl made for almost impossible odds, but that was exactly what Fargo had done, and so far he had come out ahead. That luck couldn't last, though, and he knew it. He scrambled to one side, feeling around for the gun he had dropped.

Before he could find it, the thunder of hoofbeats filled the air. A number of riders swarmed up to the campsite, and Fargo knew now he wasn't dealing with innocent prospectors.

"Get that bastard!" a man ordered, and more dark shapes charged Fargo. He straightened and met them head-on, slugging right and left as hard and fast as he could. That was all he could do.

It wasn't enough. His attackers piled on him, knocking him to the ground. Hard fists pounded him. Booted feet drove into him in vicious kicks. Pain filled Fargo's body and blurred his mind. He tried to cover up, but it was no use. They were giving him the thrashing of his life.

If they kept it up much longer, it might be the thrashing of his death.

Finally, though, the same deep, powerful voice that had ordered the men to get him called out, "That's enough! Get the son of a bitch on his feet. Let's have some light here!"

Fargo wondered where Julia was. He hoped she had had the presence of mind to slip out of the wagon and sneak off while he was fighting with the outlaws. He was certain now that these men were part of Puma Jack's gang. The one who gave the orders might be Jack himself.

Of course, even if Julia had slipped away, she probably wouldn't get far before they tracked her down. Fargo didn't want to think about what might happen to her then. It would all depend on how much control Puma Jack had over the hardcases who made up his gang.

Strong, callused hands dragged Fargo onto his feet

and held him up. Blood dripped into his eyes from a cut on his forehead. He was a mass of pain from the beating they had given him. As light flared from a makeshift torch that one of the outlaws set ablaze, he blinked the blood out of his eyes and looked around blearily.

Close to twenty men filled the little cove in the rocks where Fargo and Julia had made camp. Fargo had been so outnumbered from the start that he hadn't had a chance. He just hadn't known that when the fight started.

One of the men on horseback walked his mount forward. He wore black trousers tucked into high-topped black boots, a dark blue shirt, and a black hat. A red bandanna was tied around his neck. An ivory-handled Colt jutted up from a holster on his hip. His face was craggy and slightly lantern-jawed. He regarded Fargo with dark, intelligent eyes.

He was the leader of this band of owlhoots. Anybody could tell that just by looking at him. That made him the infamous Puma Jack, who evidently intended to be the lord of Death Valley before he was through.

"You're quite the wildcat, my friend," the horse-backer said. His voice was educated and well-modulated. "I wasn't sure if my men would be able to subdue you without killing you."

"Not . . . as big a wildcat . . . as you, Puma Jack," Fargo said thickly, through bloodied, swollen lips.

"So you know who I am," the outlaw leader said. He thumbed his hat back on his head, revealing thick white hair.

Seeing that sent a shock through Fargo. Something about Puma Jack had seemed familiar as soon as Fargo laid eyes on him. He knew he had never seen the man before, but now he understood why the bandit chieftain had stirred uneasy feelings of recognition within him.

Before Fargo could even begin to think about what this revelation meant, a shrill scream sounded from the wagon. Fargo jerked his head around, knowing that Julia hadn't slipped away and that some of Puma Jack's men had found her. As he watched, a couple of the outlaws dragged her struggling figure out of the wagon. They began to tug her forward into the glare of the torch. One of them said gleefully, "Look what we found!"

"Let go of her!" Puma Jack bellowed.

The men released Julia's arms and stepped back in surprise. Julia stumbled a little, caught her balance, and then straightened the dress she had pulled on after Fargo left the wagon. She gave her head a toss that sent her thick dark hair swirling around her shoulders. When she stepped forward so the light from the torch fell fully on her face, her chin was lifted in defiance.

"Julia!" Puma Jack exclaimed.

"Hello, Father," Julia said coolly and calmly. "Did you miss me?"

Fargo had been surprised plenty of times in his life, but seldom had he been more shocked than he was at that moment. He had briefly considered the idea that Arthur Slauson and Puma Jack might be one and the same man—after all, Slauson had gone to Death Valley approximately six months earlier, and Puma Jack had shown up in the area about the same time—but it seemed so far-fetched he had discarded it after mentioning it to Chuckwalla Smith.

Clearly, though, he had been right and it wasn't such a far-fetched notion after all. As Fargo looked from Puma Jack to Julia and back again, he could even see the family resemblance.

"What in blazes are you doing here?" Puma Jack demanded of his daughter.

"Looking for you, of course," Julia replied. She glanced at Fargo. "Skye, I'm sorry I couldn't tell you the truth. And I'm sorry that you got hurt."

"I reckon I'll live," Fargo said stiffly. To tell the truth, right now the knowledge that Julia had lied to him pained him just as much as the beating he had received. Well, almost as much, he amended.

"It wasn't all a lie, though," Julia went on. "I really did come out here with you hoping that you could help me find my father."

Puma Jack—Fargo was still having a hard time thinking of him as Arthur Slauson—swung down from his horse and motioned for his men to step back. He came forward, stood in front of Julia for a second, and then pulled her into his arms and hugged her.

"It's good to see you," he said.

"Even after you abandoned me in Los Angeles and never expected to see me again?" she asked as she stood stiffly in his embrace.

Puma Jack stepped back and put his hands on her shoulders as he frowned down at her. "I didn't abandon you," he protested. "I always figured I'd either come back for you or send for you later on."

"When?" Julia demanded.

"Well . . . once I had a big enough stake . . ."

"I've kept up with Puma Jack's activities, Father. You're quite the successful bandit. Anyway, you had plenty of money when you left me, remember? You had all that you stole from Will Bradley." She paused, then added, "And of course, you had Bradley's wife, too."

"That's none of your business," Slauson said harshly.

"You never thought anything you did was any of my business, did you? That's why you didn't have any trouble abandoning me."

Slauson glanced around. The members of his gang were all listening to the argument with his daughter, and it was clear Slauson didn't care for that.

"Tie him up and stash him somewhere," he snapped, jerking a thumb at Fargo. Then he grasped Julia's arm and half-dragged her toward the wagon. She resisted a little at first but then went with him.

As they vanished into the wagon, several of the outlaws closed in on Fargo and bound his hands behind his back. They hauled him over to the steep, rocky slope and shoved him down so that he sat against it. Then they lashed his ankles together as well.

"Sit there and keep your mouth shut," one of his captors said. "If you do that, maybe we won't have to gag you."

Fargo didn't acknowledge the order. He just stared at the wagon and wondered what Julia and her father were saying to each other in there. He knew both of them were angry.

He was pretty peeved himself. He had been used and lied to, and he never liked it when that happened. Worse, he was angry with himself for letting Julia fool him. She was a damn good actress, though, and she knew the trick of salting her lies liberally with the truth, so that they would be even more convincing.

She really had been looking for her father, and it was true he had left her in Los Angeles and come to Death Valley six months earlier. It was even true that Slauson had served in the Mexican War with Colonel Price, or else the colonel never would have helped Julia get in touch with Fargo. Slauson might have even saved Price's life. He could have been an honorable man back then, instead of the snake-blooded, murdering owlhoot that he was now.

The other outlaws had dismounted, and now they

started a fire and put a coffeepot on to boil. They didn't have to worry about being discovered; the bunch was big enough to handle any trouble that might come their way.

And this wasn't even all of them, Fargo discovered by listening to their talk. The rest of the gang had been left somewhere else, at another camp.

He leaned his head back against the rock behind him and closed his eyes. He wasn't trying to go to sleep—he hurt too much for that—but he did force his breathing into a regular pattern and tried to clear his mind. The more he rested now, the sooner he would recover from the beating.

Of course, since he was in the hands of ruthless outlaws, he might not have long to live, but that didn't matter. Fargo wasn't going to give up. Defeat wasn't in his nature. If he got a chance to fight back, he wanted to be able to make the best of it.

He wasn't sure how long he sat there before a sudden hush that fell over the camp made him open his eyes again. He looked up to see that Julia and her father had emerged from the wagon. Julia came toward him.

She knelt in front of him and gave him a solemn smile. "I'm sorry, Skye," she said. "I really am."

Fargo was in no mood to listen to her apologies, but he was curious about a couple of things. He said, "You started that fire yesterday morning hoping it would be spotted, didn't you?"

"That's right," she replied with a nod. "I thought we would run into my father and his men sooner than we did. When we didn't, I decided I would try to draw their attention."

"Do they know I'm the one who interfered when they jumped Jordan and Dailey?"

Julia threw a nervous glance back over her shoulder at the owlhoots who were gathered around the campfire. "No, and it would probably be better if you didn't say anything else about that," she said in a low voice.

"Why? They're going to kill me anyway, aren't they?"

"Actually, no. They don't have any reason to. When they fought you before, they didn't know you were with me."

"I got the feeling that you being the boss's daughter didn't carry all that much weight."

She did that defiant toss of her head and said, "You'd be surprised. My father feels guilty about leaving me behind. He'll do anything I ask, within reason. Right now I want you to be kept alive."

Fargo wondered if that was a veiled threat, as if later she might not want him alive at all but would prefer to see him dead.

"So what happens now?" he asked.

"In the morning we're going back to the main camp. My father doesn't need to have his forces split up right now."

"Why not?"

Julia smiled again. "You see, there were other things I told you the truth about, Skye. A man really did come to see me in Los Angeles, and later he and some other men did sneak into the boardinghouse hoping to kidnap me. I followed them after they left, and I found out they were working for a man named Will Bradley."

Fargo recalled her mentioning that name before. "Who's Bradley?"

"He and my father used to be partners. They were confidence men, like that sweet Gypsum talked about. They were good at it, and they made quite a bit of money over the years."

"Until your father double-crossed Bradley and stole all the loot that belonged to both of them," Fargo guessed.

"That's right," Julia confirmed.

"He stole Bradley's wife, too," Fargo went on, remembering what Julia had said earlier, "and now Bradley wants the money, and the woman, back."

"I doubt if he cares that much about Sharon. She's a slut, after all. She went willingly enough with my father. But the money . . . and revenge . . . those are different matters."

"What you're telling me," Fargo said slowly, "is that you came out here to warn your father that Bradley is on his trail."

"Exactly. If Bradley had gotten his hands on me, he would have used me as a hostage. As it is, though, I've ruined that plan, and I've alerted my father to the danger."

"He didn't know already that Bradley would come after him someday? Most of the time, if you betray a man and steal from him, he'll try to track you down and settle the score."

"Well, yes, of course, but . . ." Julia's voice trailed off and she frowned as she thought about what Fargo had just said. Her expression grew more worried as she realized the implications of it.

"That's right," Fargo said softly. "Bradley may not have known where your father was. Maybe he set you up to think you were being kidnapped and let you get away on purpose, hoping that you'd lead him straight to what he was after."

"My God," Julia breathed. "That's exactly what I've done, isn't it, Skye?"

"I reckon we'll have to wait and see," Fargo said grimly.

7

Later on toward morning, Fargo did doze off for a while, but his sleep was restless and unsatisfying. Aching from the beating he had received, bound hand and foot, and sitting on rocky ground, he had no way to truly rest.

It was after sunrise before the outlaws got ready to ride out. Julia had fed Fargo a little breakfast and held a cup so that he could sip some coffee. His hands were still bound. One of the owlhoots came over and cut his feet loose, though, so he could stand up with some help.

One of the men approached the Ovaro with Fargo's saddle, but the stallion snorted angrily and backed off, baring his teeth at the man. When the outlaw tried to come closer, the horse reared up and lashed out with his forehooves, making the man dive backward.

"Hey, boss!" the outlaw called to Arthur Slauson. "How am I supposed to saddle this crazy varmint? He won't let me get near him!"

Slauson came over to Fargo and slipped his revolver from its holster. Holding it level at his hip, he said, "If we turn you loose so you can handle your horse, are you going to try to make a break for it?"

"That would be a mite foolish, wouldn't it?" Fargo asked coldly. "I don't reckon I'd make it fifty yards before all of you blew me out of the saddle."

With a cruel grin, Slauson said, "That's exactly what would happen. I'm glad to see you're smart enough to know that." He jerked his free hand at one of his men. "Cut him loose."

A moment later, Fargo's hands were free. Pain stabbed into them as the blood began to flow again. He rubbed some circulation back into them, then took the saddle and approached the Ovaro. The stallion was still a little skittish because of all the strangers around, but he allowed Fargo to put the blanket and saddle on him.

Fargo's Colt, Henry rifle, and Arkansas Toothpick were all gone, having been confiscated by the outlaws. He asked, "Can I have my hat back? It'll be mighty hot out in the sun later in the day without it."

"Sure," Slauson replied. "Julia, get your friend's hat and give it to him."

Julia fetched the hat from the wagon and brought it to Fargo. As he took it from her, he said, "Thanks." Lowering his voice, he added, "Your father doesn't know who I am, does he?"

"He thinks you're just someone I hired as a guide," she replied, equally quietly.

"Let's go," Slauson called over to them, evidently not noticing the brief conversation between Fargo and Julia.

Julia went back to the wagon. Fargo stepped up into the saddle. Most of the outlaws were mounted now and ready to ride out. The others hurriedly got on their horses, not wanting to risk the wrath of Puma Jack.

Several of the men fell in closely around Fargo, forming a guard detail. One of them spat and said, "I ain't sure why we're keepin' you alive, mister."

Fargo noticed a large bruise on the man's face and wondered if he was one of the men who had fought with him the night before. That would explain his hostility.

"You're keeping me alive because that's what your boss wants," Fargo said.

"It ain't what he wants so much as it is what that gal wants," another outlaw put in with a sneer. "How's it feel to have a woman save your life?"

"Better than being dead," Fargo said.

They couldn't argue with that, so they didn't say anything else.

With a wave of his arm, Slauson led the gang away from the campsite. He rode alongside the wagon, and the rest of the owlhoots trailed behind.

The group headed north, moving farther out toward the salt flats than the route Fargo and Julia had used. Fargo glanced back at the hills and the canyons he had searched for Arthur Slauson. He had found Slauson . . . or rather, Slauson had found him. Things hadn't worked out exactly the way Fargo had hoped they would.

The temperature rose and became uncomfortable. The men riding with Fargo grumbled about the heat. One of them said, "We should've laid low back there and ridden at night."

"The boss wants to get back to Furnace Creek, I reckon," another outlaw replied.

Fargo knew that Furnace Creek was on the eastern side of Death Valley. He had already noticed that they were following one of the old trails that had been used for centuries by Indians and animals, especially the coyotes. Anyone who was lost in Death Valley could follow one of those trails if he was lucky enough to find one, knowing that it would lead him to water.

The heat grew almost unbearable as the riders moved out onto the salt flats. Sunlight reflected off the white crust that covered the ground, nearly blinding them and making it even hotter. The outlaw who had said they should have waited for night before attempting this had been right. Crossing the worst of

Death Valley in the middle of the day was a good way to fry.

But this was also one of the places where the valley was the narrowest. The Funeral Mountains loomed in front of the riders, appearing so close in the clear air that it seemed the men could reach out and touch them.

Fargo had crossed deserts before, including the brutal *Jornada del Muerte*—the Journey of Death— over in New Mexico Territory. He knew that men could stand more than they thought they could. And with the coyote trail that marked the shortest route across the salt flats to follow, they could make it before they were overcome by heat and thirst.

Still, he was damned glad when they left the flats behind and started climbing slightly toward the mountains. Blotches of green up ahead in the hills marked the springs along Furnace Creek. This was in many ways the most hospitable part of Death Valley, so it came as no surprise that the gang made their headquarters here.

A short time later the riders came to the dry creek bed. The stream ran only during the occasional rains. Fargo recalled hearing that once there had come a cloudburst so strong that Furnace Creek had flooded. It was hard to believe there could ever be that much water here in this arid inferno.

They followed the creek bed higher into the hills, then branched off along a wash. Soon the walls of the wash rose high enough to provide some welcome shade. Fargo was looking up at one of those walls when he caught the glint of sunlight off metal.

Somebody was up there with a gun. Fargo saw Slauson glance in the same direction and give a slight nod of satisfaction. The outlaw leader had spotted the reflection, too, which meant he had been expecting it.

At least one sentry was up there, guarding the

wash. That was enough to tell Fargo they were fast approaching the gang's hideout.

Scrub brush became more common, and here and there were patches of sparse grass. The vegetation was evidence there was freshwater fairly close to the surface.

As the group rounded a bend, with Slauson and the wagon still at its head, they came in sight of a veritable oasis in the wilderness. A pool of water some twenty feet across sparkled in the sunshine. Several small trees grew around it. The men had to hold their horses back to keep them from bolting toward the oasis.

Beyond the pool, a creek meandered down the center of the wash for a ways before curving and climbing into a blind canyon where the spring that fed it would be located. A small cabin sat beside the creek, made out of logs from trees cut higher in the Funeral Mountains. There was a pole corral, too, along with several tents.

The outlaws were home.

Several hard-faced men came forward to greet the newcomers. Fargo knew from listening to the talk among the gang that only six or eight men had been left here to hold down the fort while Slauson and the rest of the outlaws went to see who had dared to venture into Death Valley. The owlhoots who had stayed behind greeted their companions and looked curiously at the wagon—and at the beautiful young woman driving it.

As they all came to a halt, one of Fargo's guards bumped his horse into the Ovaro, drawing an angry snort from the stallion.

"Get down off o' there," the man ordered. "But don't try anything funny."

"Farthest thing from my mind," Fargo said as he swung a leg over the saddle and stepped down to the ground.

As he stood there holding the Ovaro's reins, he glanced toward the cabin and saw a woman standing in the doorway. She was relatively young, though older than Julia, and had black hair that fell to her shoulders. She wore boots, men's trousers, and a buckskin shirt.

If this was the woman Chuckwalla had seen with Puma Jack, Fargo understood how the old pelican had mistaken Julia for her. They were about the same size and both had dark hair.

That would be Sharon Bradley, Fargo thought, the wife of Slauson's former partner in crime who had run off with Slauson. She was quite attractive, and no matter what Julia had said, Fargo figured Sharon was one more reason Will Bradley would want to catch up to Slauson.

The outlaw leader helped Julia down from the wagon, then took her arm and led her over to the cabin, where they spoke to Sharon. Fargo couldn't hear what was said, but from the looks on their faces, Fargo figured there was an instinctive dislike between the two women.

That was interesting, and knowing about it might come in handy later on, Fargo told himself.

Julia and Sharon went inside the cabin. Slauson turned, pointed at Fargo, and ordered, "Bring him in here." Then he followed the women into the cabin.

One of the outlaws said, "You heard the boss" and gave Fargo a hard shove that sent him stumbling forward. Fargo caught his balance and walked toward the cabin. Several of the owlhoots followed him, guns drawn.

When he stepped inside, he found that the cabin had only one room, with a bunk along the wall and a rough table and chairs in the center of the floor. A woodburning stove sat in the corner, cold at the moment.

Slauson and Julia sat at the table. Slauson had a

jug in front of him. Sharon Bradley stood to one side, looking a little uncomfortable.

Slauson gestured at the chair opposite him and said to Fargo, "Sit down."

Fargo took a seat. He didn't know what was going to happen here, but if he waited, he was sure he would find out.

Slauson pushed the jug toward him. "Have a drink."

"Don't mind if I do," Fargo said. "That was a mighty thirsty ride across the salt flats."

He uncorked the jug and tipped it to his mouth, pausing just long enough for the smell coming from it to confirm that it held whiskey. He swallowed a mouthful. It cut the dust just fine and started a warm glow in his belly.

"Who the hell are you, mister?" Slauson asked.

Fargo glanced at Julia as he set the jug back on the table. "Didn't your daughter tell you?"

"Just that she hired you in Blackwater to be her guide through Death Valley. Said your name was Smith, Chuckwalla Smith."

Fargo smiled faintly. It had been quick thinking on Julia's part not to identify him as Skye Fargo, although he thought she might have come up with something better than using the old prospector's name.

"That's right," he said. "That's who I am."

"I never heard of Chuckwalla Smith," Slauson said.

"I never heard of Puma Jack until a few days ago," Fargo shot back.

Slauson's eyes narrowed. "Well, you've sure as hell heard of me now, haven't you?" Without waiting for an answer, he went on. "What do you suppose I ought to do with you, Smith?"

"Thank me for helping your daughter and let me go on my way?" Fargo suggested, still smiling.

"Now that you've seen this place? I don't think that would be a very good idea."

"Why not?" Fargo leaned forward and grew more solemn. "I don't care what you're doing up here, Slauson. It's none of my business. Julia paid me to help her find her father. I did that. As far as I'm concerned, the job's over. I'm harmless."

"The way you fought last night, you didn't seem too harmless," Slauson pointed out.

"Your men jumped me, remember? I was just defending myself. I didn't know who they were or what was going on."

Slauson reached out, snagged the jug, and took a drink. "What's going on," he said as he thumped the jug back down on the table, "is that I'm taking over Death Valley, lock, stock, and barrel."

"What about all the prospectors?"

"What do I care about a bunch of desert rats?" Slauson asked with a dismissive wave of his hand. "They can either get out or die. Doesn't matter to me one way or the other as long as they're gone."

Fargo knew that Slauson's gang had already killed several of the prospectors, but he didn't say anything about that. Instead he said, "You want any gold and silver that's up here for yourself."

Slauson snorted. "There's not enough gold or silver for me to worry about it. What I want is a place where my men and I can hole up between jobs. There are a lot of lawmen looking for us already, and there'll be more when we pull some of the jobs I have in mind. Death Valley is our sanctuary."

"Well, you don't have to worry about me," Fargo insisted. "I don't give a damn what you've done or what your plans are. I'm no friend to the law, either."

"Oh, a hardcase, eh?"

Fargo shrugged. Let Slauson believe whatever he wanted to.

After a moment, the bandit chief went on. "You know, I'm starting to believe you, Smith. But a man in my business can't be too careful. I can't just trust that you won't run to the law as soon as we let you go."

"I'm telling you—"

Slauson held up a hand to stop him. "No, the only way I'm going to trust you is if you have something to lose, too. Ride with us for a while, and then, if you still want to leave, you'll be a wanted man, too. You'll have to steer clear of the law then."

The offer took Fargo somewhat by surprise, although he had wondered if Slauson might not be leading up to something like that. Julia and Sharon hadn't been expecting it, either, to judge by the looks on their faces.

"I'm not sure that's a good idea—" Julia began.

"And you're not in charge here, either," Slauson cut in sharply. "I'm offering your friend Smith a chance to save his life. If he's not interested . . . well, there are plenty of buzzards and coyotes out here who are always in need of a meal."

"I didn't say I wasn't interested," Fargo said slowly. "In fact, it's a pretty appealing idea."

"Nothing like the prospect of dying to make a man see the light of reason," Slauson said. He took another drink and shoved the jug back to Fargo. "Have a drink on it."

Fargo downed another slug of whiskey. Wary of a trick, he asked, "What makes you think you can trust me just because I go along with your proposition?"

"I'm not a fool. You won't get your guns back until we're ready to ride out on our next job. If you try anything fancy between now and then, you won't live very long. Somebody will be watching you all the time."

"But if I cooperate, you'll give me my guns and let me ride with you?"

"That's what I just said, isn't it?" Slauson demanded a little impatiently.

Fargo glanced at Julia. Her lips were pressed together tightly, and he couldn't read the look in her eyes. Clearly, she was leaving the decision up to him.

"You've got yourself a deal," Fargo said. "And you won't be disappointed, Puma Jack."

"I'd better not be," Slauson said, "because if I am, you won't live very long, my friend."

Slauson ordered his men to take Fargo back out and decide which tent he was going to share. Fargo could tell that the outlaws weren't happy about having his company forced on them, but none of them were going to argue with Puma Jack. It was obvious he ruled this gang with an iron fist.

One of the men who had guarded him on the ride to the hideout said in a surly voice, "I reckon you can stay with Jimmy and me. But I'm warnin' you, you're on a mighty short rein. Don't go wanderin' around, or you're liable to get shot."

"I'm not looking for trouble," Fargo said.

"Maybe not, but some o' these boys are, especially the ones you whaled on last night." The man wiped the back of his hand across his nose. "Name's Mac, by the way."

"Pleased to meet you, Mac."

"No, you ain't. You wish you'd never laid eyes on any of us."

"You might be surprised about that," Fargo said honestly.

His brain was working feverishly. He had dodged death, but only for the time being. He wasn't going to join this gang of desperadoes, no matter what he had told Slauson. But right now all he could do was play for time and hope to figure out some way to bring an end to their reign of terror in Death Valley.

Ignoring the hostile glares that some of the other men sent his way, Fargo followed Mac and Jimmy to one of the tents pitched along the creek bank. Mac was an older man with plenty of gray in his hair, a veteran rider of the owlhoot trails. Jimmy was younger, not much more than a kid, with freckles and a shock of red hair.

"We'll be watchin' you all the time," Jimmy said, letting his hand rest on the butt of his gun.

"That's fine," Fargo said. "I'm not going anywhere."

As if to prove it, he sat down under one of the trees, stretched his legs out in front of him, and leaned his back against the trunk. When he tipped his hat down over his eyes, anybody watching him would think that he didn't have a care in the world.

That was wrong, of course. Despite his idle appearance, as he sat there his eyes moved constantly, roving around the hideout, taking in all the details, memorizing what was where. When he finally did make a move, he probably wouldn't have the luxury of hesitating.

Mac and Jimmy sat down beside the tent and rolled quirlies. As they smoked, their narrow-eyed gazes never strayed much from Fargo.

After a while, Julia emerged from the cabin and walked toward the creek. When she came up to the two outlaws, she said, "I want to talk to Mr. Smith . . . alone."

"Puma Jack told us to watch him," Mac objected.

"And you can, from over there where you can't eavesdrop," Julia replied, pointing toward the other tents. "Or should I go ask my father why you're not cooperating with me?"

Mac threw his cigarette down disgustedly. "Lady, we'll go along with what you say . . . this time . . . but you better remember that we ride for your pa, not for you." He stood up. "Come on, Jimmy."

Glaring, the young redhead followed the older outlaw. They went to a spot along the creek where the other men were watering their horses. Fargo couldn't hear the low-voiced conversation that went on, but judging by the angry looks cast in their direction, he was willing to bet that they were complaining about the boss's high-handed daughter.

Julia stood in front of Fargo and said, "What are you doing, Skye?"

"Trying to stay alive."

"You know you're not going to join the gang."

"Don't be so sure of that," Fargo told her. "I've gotten fond of breathing."

She shook her head. "I haven't known you for very long, but I know you better than that. Skye Fargo would never turn outlaw."

"I'm not Skye Fargo anymore. I'm Chuckwalla Smith, remember?" He couldn't help but chuckle a little. "It's a good thing none of these boys know the real Chuckwalla. I don't think I could pass for an old prospector."

Julia didn't seem to find the situation amusing. She said, "What are you going to do?"

"Wait and see what happens," Fargo told her honestly.

"You're going to betray my father to the law, aren't you?"

"There's no law around here," Fargo pointed out. "And if you were so worried about what I might do, why did you lie for me in the first place?"

"Because I didn't . . ." She looked around miserably. "Because I didn't want to see you get hurt. You mean too much to me. But my father means more, and I won't just stand by and see him hurt, either. You need to remember that, Skye."

"I intend to."

"We'll let things ride for now. Just don't force me to choose between the two of you."

105

With a look that was a mixture of wariness and affection, Julia turned away and walked back to the cabin. Mac and Jimmy returned from the creek.

"You done talkin' to your little friend?" Jimmy asked with a sneer.

"I don't know if she's my friend or not," Fargo said, and he meant every word of it.

During the rest of the hot afternoon, everybody found whatever shade they could and took it easy. Julia avoided Fargo. She probably didn't want her father to think there was anything serious between them. He wondered what she had told Slauson about the private conversation she'd had with him earlier.

Over the next twenty-four hours, Mac and Jimmy were never far from Fargo. He ignored them for the most part. They shared their tent and their food with him, a little grudgingly, and took turns sleeping so that at least one of them was always awake to watch Fargo. He didn't give them any reason to be suspicious of him.

Late in the afternoon of the second day in the outlaw hideout, Sharon Bradley walked over to the tree where Fargo was spending most of his time. She said to Mac and Jimmy, "Jack wants to see you two."

They didn't argue this time as they had with Julia the day before. Instead they stood up, abandoning the poker hand they'd been playing with a deck of greasy cards, and walked quickly toward the cabin. Mac asked over his shoulder, "You gonna keep an eye on him while we're gone?"

Sharon waved a hand to indicate that she would. She lowered the hand and let it rest on the butt of the pistol she wore holstered at her waist. Not very many women carried a gun like that, but Sharon looked like she knew how to use it. And there were a couple of dozen hardcases within easy earshot if she needed help, too.

"How are you doing, Mr. Smith?" she asked quietly.

"All right," Fargo replied with a nod. He sensed that Sharon wanted something, but he had no idea what it might be.

She didn't make him wait long to find out. She dropped her voice even more and said, "I was in Santa Fe last year. A man rode by on the street, a very handsome man on a black-and-white horse. When I asked someone who he was, they told me his name was Skye Fargo, sometimes called the Trailsman."

Fargo tensed. His muscles were ready for action if he had to spring to his feet and make a run for it. He knew he wouldn't get very far, but if he could just get his hands on a gun . . .

"You bear a certain resemblance to that man, Mr. Smith," Sharon went on. "Would your real name happen to be Skye Fargo?"

"Julia told you, I'm Chuckwalla Smith."

Sharon's blue eyes glittered with anger. "I know what that little bitch said. I don't trust her, though. She would say anything, tell any lie, to get her father to do what she wants him to do."

"What is it you want, ma'am?" Fargo asked.

"Ma'am," Sharon repeated. She gave a hollow laugh. "Nobody has been that respectful toward me since I left my husband and came out here with Jack. They all know I'm his slut."

Fargo frowned. "I don't like to hear any woman talked about like that, even when she's doing it herself."

"Well, you're an unusual man, Mr. Smith. Or should I say Mr. Fargo? You never did answer my question."

Fargo didn't say anything.

"Don't worry," Sharon went on after a moment. "The last thing I want to do is give your secret away. You see, I need your help."

"Help for what?"

Her voice broke slightly as she said, "To get away from here."

8

Fargo kept his face impassive. He suspected a trick by Slauson. Maybe the outlaw leader had tumbled to his prisoner's true identity.

Or maybe Sharon was telling the truth. Until he knew for sure, Fargo wasn't going to walk into a trap.

"Maybe you'd better explain what you mean," he suggested.

Sharon looked like she was about to, but before she could go on, Julia emerged from the cabin and walked toward them. Fargo saw the look of dislike that went across Sharon's face. It was almost outright hatred.

Julia's expression wasn't any friendlier when she looked at Sharon. Clearly, these two women were jealous of each other and their relationships with Arthur "Puma Jack" Slauson.

"I'll watch Smith now," Julia said as she came up. "You can go back inside."

"It's not any trouble—" Sharon began.

"You'd better go," Julia cut in. "My father might need you."

Sharon hesitated a moment longer, then shrugged. "Sure. I was just standing here keeping an eye on this friend of yours." She walked toward the cabin, her back stiff.

"I never did like that bitch," Julia hissed as she watched Sharon go.

Fargo could have told her that the feeling was mutual, but instead he kept quiet and waited to see what else Julia had to say.

"What did she want?"

"She was just watching me because Mac and Jimmy had to go talk to your father."

"It looked like she was talking to you about something."

Fargo shrugged. "Just passing the time of day. Talking about how hot it is."

Julia frowned, but she didn't press the issue.

Fargo did a little prodding of his own by asking, "How come the two of you don't get along?"

"I just don't trust her. She betrayed her husband, after all. What's to stop her from betraying my father?"

"Well, that's one way to look at it," Fargo allowed. "How long were your father and Will Bradley partners?"

"I'm not sure. Several years, at least. I lived with my mother until about four years ago, and Father and Will were already working together then and had been for quite a while."

She seemed to want to talk, so Fargo sat there with an interested expression on his face, clearly waiting for her to go on. That was enough encouragement.

"You know, I should have expected that he would abandon me. He abandoned my mother, after all. Just up and left her in Kansas City with a child to raise. Oh, he sent money to us and visited every now and then, but we never knew where he was or what he was doing. He just showed up for a day or two; then he would be gone again."

"Must have been difficult for your mother," Fargo commented.

"I'm sure it was. It aged her before her time, I know that. I helped as much as I could, but there was only so much I could do." Julia sighed. "After

110

Mother got sick and died, Father showed up. He must have had someone keeping an eye on us, because he knew she was gone. He took me with him when he left again."

"What did the two of you do?"

She gave that distinctive toss of her head. "I was eighteen years old and beautiful, if I do say so myself. What do you think we did?" Without waiting for Fargo to answer, she went on. "We swindled people, mostly men, and we were damned good at it."

A faint smile tugged at the corners of Fargo's mouth. "I'll bet you were a natural."

"Yes, I was. We would have done just fine without Will and Sharon, but Will was my father's partner, and he showed more loyalty to him than he ever had to his family . . . at least for a while."

"And you said Sharon never liked you?"

Julia smiled. "I said *I* never liked *her*. But she felt the same way. She hated me, in fact, because of her husband."

"You and Bradley . . . ?"

"Will would have liked that, but no, he never managed to do anything except get me alone a time or two and try to kiss me. Sharon caught us one of those times, though, and took it wrong. She thought I was trying to seduce Will. She told me later to stay away from him, or she would kill me. Will, of course, let her think it was all my fault."

"I can see why the two of you aren't friends," Fargo said dryly. "What happened to break it all up?"

"Nothing in particular. I guess my father was just waiting until they had enough money to make stealing the whole pot worthwhile. That happened up in San Francisco. When I realized that Father and Sharon were gone and knew what had happened, I got out of town before Will could get his hands on me. I knew he'd be wild with rage. I worked my way down to Los Angeles, and it took him a while to catch up to me. I guess he figured that sooner or later I'd lead him to Father. Which, of course, is exactly what I've done."

"Maybe, maybe not," Fargo said. "We don't know for sure about that."

"You're right, there hasn't been any sign of him yet. Maybe I really gave them the slip. Maybe my father wins again." Her laugh was humorless. "He always does, one way or another."

After a moment or two of silence, Fargo said, "How did he wind up leading a gang of outlaws? You said he was a confidence man before. That's not usually what folks think of as a desperado."

"As a young man he grew up on the Natchez Trace. You've heard of it?"

Fargo nodded. A few decades earlier, the Natchez Trace had been the roughest part of the road between Natchez, Mississippi, and Nashville, Tennessee, teeming with murderers and highwaymen. In those days, more throats were cut along the Natchez Trace than anywhere else in the young, wild country.

"He was a thief and a killer while he was still just a boy. That was where he got the name Puma Jack, in fact. So by becoming an outlaw, he was just returning to his roots, I suppose you could say. He's always been a natural leader, and he's ruthless enough not to let anyone stand in his way."

"Sounds almost like you admire him."

"I admire him . . . and I despise him. I love him . . . he's my father, after all . . . and I hate him for . . . for what he did to my mother . . . and for taking me in and then deserting me for that . . . that whore . . ." Julia shook her head. "I don't know what I think or what I feel anymore, Skye."

"Chuckwalla," Fargo reminded her quietly.

Her head jerked in a nod. "Yes, of course. Have

you . . . have you figured out what you're going to do?"

"Not really. What do you think I ought to do?"

She came closer to him and lowered her voice even more. "I've been thinking about it. I want to help you get away. After you're gone, I'll tell my father who you really are and warn him that he'll have to leave Death Valley before you have time to lead a posse back here."

"He won't like that," Fargo told her.

"No, of course not. But there won't be anything he can do about it."

"Except maybe kill you," Fargo said bluntly.

"No. He would never do that, no matter what."

"You'd better be mighty certain about that, because you'd be wagering your life."

"I know. I'm certain."

"How about this?" Fargo suggested. "You help both of us escape, and you come with me back to Blackwater."

She shook her head. "I can't do that. Now that I've found him, I have to stay with him."

"You're sure about that?"

"Positive. I'm sorry, Sk—Chuckwalla."

Fargo hadn't expected her to agree to his proposal, but he'd had to try. He had his doubts that Julia could actually help him escape, but he was willing to play along with her for the time being, at least until he found out what Sharon Bradley had in mind. Unlike Julia, she evidently wanted out of here.

Fargo inclined his head toward the cabin. "My keepers are coming back." Mac and Jimmy had come out of the cabin and were walking toward them. "We'll talk again later."

Julia nodded.

She swung around to greet the two outlaws by asking, "What did my father want?"

Mac glowered. "He read us the riot act about sassin' you. You been complainin' about us since yesterday, gal?"

"I just think you need to treat me with a little more respect," Julia said haughtily.

Jimmy tugged his hat off, exposing his red hair. "We're sorry, ma'am," he said, and he sounded sincere. Fargo wondered if he had finally tumbled to the fact that Julia was a beautiful young woman and decided that he ought to be playing up to her instead of resenting her. "We'll try to be a mite nicer, won't we, Mac?"

Mac just grunted. He was old enough to be largely immune to Julia's charms. Although any man still drawing breath would never be completely unmoved by the presence of a woman like Julia, Fargo thought.

She went back to the cabin, and he resumed his casual pose leaning against the tree with his hat tipped forward. He had learned quite a bit today and would mull it over while he was waiting to see what would happen next.

Somehow, he had a feeling that it wouldn't take long before events broke again.

That evening, before supper, Sharon Bradley came over and said to Fargo, "You're eating with us tonight."

"Good," Mac said. "I don't like givin' this fella any of our grub."

Fargo ignored the outlaw and got to his feet. As he walked toward the cabin with Sharon, he said quietly, "I've been thinking about what you said earlier."

"Well, just forget about it," she replied tightly. "I made a mistake. I was a damned fool."

"Why? Because you think Slauson will never let you go?"

114

"He won't. He'd kill me first." Sharon swallowed. "With that bitch of a daughter poisoning him against me, he's liable to kill me anyway."

"All the more reason for you to get out of here," Fargo said. "I'd help you, if you helped me."

She glanced over at him, but she didn't say any more. They were at the cabin. Sharon motioned for Fargo to go in first.

The place was lit by a lantern on the table. Slauson and Julia already sat there. Fargo and Sharon joined them. The atmosphere inside the cabin was tense.

The meal consisted of beans with chunks of salt pork floating in them, along with cornbread and coffee. Rough fare, but pretty good, Fargo thought as he dug in. Nobody talked much. When they were finished, Sharon cleared the table.

Slauson took a couple of cigars from his pocket and slid one of them across the table to Fargo. Fargo took it and bit the end off. He smoked only occasionally, but he thought it would be a good idea to go along with Slauson for now. The man might talk and reveal more of his plans over the cigars.

Julia got a burning twig from the fire and lit both cigars. Slauson puffed on his, blew out a cloud of smoke contentedly, and looked across at Fargo. ·

"From what I've seen and heard, you've been behaving yourself just fine, Smith."

"I told you, I don't have anything against you, Puma Jack," Fargo said. "I'll still ride away if you'll let me, or I'll stay here and join your gang. Your call."

"You're an accommodating sort. I'll give you that."

Fargo smiled thinly. "Just the sort who wants to stay alive."

Slauson inclined his head toward Julia. "You have an ardent defender in my daughter. She seems to think quite highly of you."

"I'm glad to hear that."

"While you were bringing her out here, did anything more go on than just guiding?"

"Father!" Julia exclaimed, blushing. "You don't have any call to imply things like that. Mr. Smith was a perfect gentleman."

"There's no such thing," Slauson growled. "No matter what sort of façade he puts up, every man is an animal under the skin. You'd do well to remember that, Julia."

"Another of your lessons, Father, like how to spot a potential victim and swindle him out of everything he has?"

Rather than looking embarrassed, Slauson grinned widely and said, "That's right. If you listen to me, girl, you'll never be surprised or disappointed by human nature, because you'll know that man is capable of anything." He turned his head and said to Sharon, "Get the jug."

She brought it over to the table. Fargo and Slauson smoked their cigars and passed the jug back and forth. Fargo had a pleasant glow in his belly from the whiskey, but it didn't muddle his thinking any.

"What is it you want with me, Slauson?" he asked.

Slauson leaned forward, rested his elbows on the table, and regarded Fargo intently. "I want to figure you out," he said. "You seem like more than just some saddle tramp. If I didn't know better, I'd say you might be a lawman, or a military officer."

Fargo shook his head. "I'm neither of those things. You have my word on that."

He was telling the truth, as far as it went. Although he had worked closely with the army on numerous occasions, it had always been as a civilian. And even though he had worn a lawman's badge a few times in the past, it had been a while since he'd packed a star.

He couldn't tell if Slauson was convinced or not.

The boss outlaw rolled his cigar from one side of his mouth to the other and grunted noncommittally. He stood up and said, "Come on."

"Where are we going?" Fargo asked as he came to his feet.

"I'm taking you back over to Mac and Jimmy."

Sharon said, "Why don't you let me do that, Jack?"

Fargo thought she might want to talk to him some more about escaping from Slauson and the rest of the gang.

But Slauson shook his head and said, "No, you stay here with Julia."

"Father—" Julia began.

Slauson picked up his hat and put it on. "Do like I say, both of you. Come on, Smith."

When they were outside with the door of the cabin closed behind them, Slauson sighed and said, "You ever find yourself in a den with two badgers, Smith?"

"Can't say as I have," Fargo replied.

"Well, that would probably be better than being in a cabin with two women who hate each other. Count your blessings."

"Small words of comfort to a condemned man."

Slauson's cigar tilted up at a jaunty angle. "Hell, you're not condemned. In fact, I'm coming around to the idea of letting you ride with us for a while. For as long as you want, if you're good enough."

"How will you know that until I go on a job with you?"

"I won't, at least not for sure," Slauson admitted. "But I can get an idea from watching how you handle yourself. That's why I lied to the women. I'm not taking you back to your tent. I've arranged for a little test instead."

Uneasiness prickled the hair on the back of Fargo's neck. "A test?" he repeated.

"That's right." Slauson raised his voice and called to the other outlaws, "Come on in, boys."

They gathered quickly around Fargo and Slauson until Fargo found himself completely ringed by desperadoes. Now he knew that Slauson was up to something, and he was equally certain that it wouldn't be anything good.

"It's time for you to prove yourself, Smith," Slauson said.

"How do I do that?"

Slauson crooked a finger and one of the outlaws stepped forward—a burly, bearded man in a poncho.

"Stay alive against Rufe here," Slauson said. "He likes to break a fella's neck and then twist it right off his shoulders."

"Yeah," the outlaw called Rufe said in a rumbling voice. "I do."

"Trial by fire, eh?" Fargo said.

"You could call it that. I prefer to think of it as survival of the fittest."

"A fight to the death, then?" Fargo wanted to know.

"Not really. Rufe is allowed to kill you, if he can, but I can't afford to lose him. Make sure he stays alive, Smith. If he dies, you'll be dead five seconds later."

"Seems to me like the deck's stacked against me," Fargo said tautly.

"Just like everything else in life." Slauson nodded curtly and stepped back. "Get to it."

Rufe took his broad-brimmed hat off and handed it to one of the other outlaws, then started to pull his poncho over his head.

Fargo didn't wait. Even though it went against the grain to strike while his opponent wasn't ready, he launched himself forward and aimed a kick at Rufe's groin.

The big man twisted aside and took the kick on his meaty thigh, roaring in pain and anger as he did so. As he tried to jerk the poncho over his head, it got tangled and hung there, blinding him for a moment. Fargo used that time to hammer in a couple of punches, a left to the belly and a right over the heart.

Rufe seemed to barely feel the blows. They didn't stagger him—that was for sure. He finally tore the poncho off his head and charged toward Fargo like a runaway freight train.

Fargo dove out of the way, trailing a leg behind him so that Rufe would stumble over it. Rufe cursed sulfurously as he stumbled and went to his hands and knees. Fargo rolled over and came up on his feet in one smooth, agile move. The toe of his boot thudded into Rufe's ribs and sent the big man sprawling.

By now the outlaws gathered around were roaring their encouragement to Rufe. Slauson called to Fargo, "You fight dirty!"

Fargo paused just long enough to respond, "Like a man fighting to stay alive!" Then he went after Rufe again.

This time Rufe was ready for him, though. The big man's hands shot up and grabbed Fargo's ankle. With a grunt and a heave, he sent Fargo flying through the air.

Some of the outlaws who had been crowding in close scattered as Fargo came toward them. He hit the ground hard and rolled over a couple of times. Half-stunned, he lay there for a second, until the rush of feet warned him that Rufe was coming after him now.

Fargo pushed himself over onto his back and lifted both legs as Rufe leaped at him. The heels of Fargo's boots dug into Rufe's belly, causing the breath to explode from the big man's mouth. Bracing himself against the ground, Fargo used his legs to lever Rufe up and over him.

The men who were in Rufe's path didn't have time to get out of his way. With a wild yell and flailing arms and legs, Rufe sailed through the air and crashed into several of the outlaws. All of them went down in a tangle.

That gave Fargo time to get back to his feet. With his heart pounding and his chest heaving, he stood there waiting to see if Rufe was going to get up.

Somehow, he wasn't surprised at all when the big man lumbered up from the ground, shaking his head like a bull, and roared out his anger. Rufe came at him again, but not in a wild, out-of-control charge this time. Instead, Rufe swung his fists in looping, sledgehammer blows, any one of which might take Fargo's head off if it connected solidly.

Fargo blocked some of the punches and avoided others, ducking and weaving so that the blows that landed only grazed him. Even those glancing blows packed enough power so that his ears rang and his head was spinning. He was so busy defending himself from the flurry of punches that he couldn't launch an attack of his own.

It was only a matter of time, he thought, before Rufe knocked him down and out, and that would be the end of it. Rufe would stomp the life out of him. He had to end the fight somehow before it came to that.

As Fargo ducked and let one of Rufe's hamlike fists go over his head, he lunged forward and wrapped his arms around the big man's thighs. With all the power of his legs behind the driving tackle, Fargo was able to force Rufe back a couple of steps. Rufe yelled in alarm as Fargo took him off his feet. He slammed down on his back.

Fargo pounced on top of his opponent, coming down with a knee in Rufe's groin. This time Rufe wasn't able to avoid it. He howled in pain from the crushing blow. The agony he was in distracted him long enough for Fargo to grab his head, tangling his fingers in Rufe's long hair. Fargo jerked Rufe's head up and then brought it down hard on the ground.

He did that twice more before Rufe finally went limp underneath him. Satisfied that his brutish foe was unconscious at last, Fargo pushed himself up and staggered back. With his fists clenched, he looked around to see if any of the other owlhoots were going to attack him.

Some of them looked like they wanted to, but they weren't going to make a move without their leader telling them to. And Slauson was coming forward casually to congratulate Fargo on his triumph.

"That was quite a battle," Slauson said as he clapped a hand on Fargo's shoulder. "No one's ever beaten Rufe hand to hand before. You can take care of yourself, Smith."

Fargo bent to pick up his hat, which had fallen off during the fracas. He punched the crown back into shape and settled it on his head.

"And I still haven't recovered completely from that beating your boys gave me a couple of nights ago," he said.

Slauson threw his head back and laughed. "That's right. I'd forgotten about that. I suppose Rufe is lucky you weren't at full strength."

Fargo didn't say anything. To tell the truth, he was having trouble staying on his feet. He felt dizzy and as weak as a newborn kitten.

But he wasn't going to let Slauson see that. Instead, he maintained his stoic façade until Slauson finally said, "Come on back to the cabin. You're pretty banged up. Sharon can take a look at you. She's pretty good at patching up injuries."

Fargo didn't argue. As the rest of the gang dispersed and several of the men dragged the unconscious Rufe toward one of the tents, Fargo went with Slauson back to the cabin.

The two women were standing just outside the door, on opposite sides of the opening. Clearly, both of them had been watching the fight between Fargo and Rufe. Julia stepped forward with an anxious expression on her face, and Fargo hoped fervently that her concern for him wouldn't make her forget and call him Skye.

She didn't. She said, "Are you all right, Mr. Smith?"

"Reckon I will be," Fargo said. "That is, if people ever stop trying to kill me for a while."

"You don't have to worry about that," Slauson said. "Sharon, take Mr. Smith inside and tend to his cuts and bruises."

She nodded and motioned for Fargo to go first, then followed him inside. Slauson and Julia stayed outside, talking quietly. Fargo could hear them through the open door but couldn't make out the words.

He sat down, grateful that he could get off his feet before he fell down, and took off his hat. He put it on the table and took a deep breath, feeling a twinge in his side where one of Rufe's punches had landed. He hoped it was just a bruise and not a cracked rib.

Sharon wet a rag from some water in a bucket and came over to the table. She stood in front of Fargo and dabbed at the cuts and scratches and scrapes on his face. When he winced a little, she said quietly, "Sorry."

"That's all right," he told her. Even in his battered state, he was well aware of how her full breasts thrust out against the buckskin shirt right in front of his face. He tilted his head back slightly so that he could look up at her.

Though her face showed some of the strain of the hard living she had done, she was still a mighty handsome woman, he thought. Those eyes were so blue they were like mountain pools in which a man could lose himself. Her lips were full and inviting.

She was another man's woman, though, and not

just any man, but a ruthless outlaw who led a whole gang of bloody-handed bandits.

But she wanted out of Death Valley, Fargo reminded himself, and she might just be his ticket out as well.

"Have you thought any more about what you said to me earlier?" he asked her, pitching his voice low enough that the question wouldn't be overheard outside.

"I told you," she hissed. "That was a mistake."

"You're afraid of Slauson. I don't reckon I blame you. But I can help you, if you'll help me."

She looked sharply at him. "How do I know I can trust you?"

"How do I know I can trust you?"

As a matter of fact, Fargo did trust her. If her original approach to him had been false, a trick orchestrated by Slauson to trap him, then Sharon wouldn't have pulled back later like she had. If treachery was her goal, she would have encouraged Fargo to make escape plans, rather than changing her mind about it.

Unless she was playing a deeper game than Fargo thought she was . . .

"If he catches us plotting against him, he'll kill us both," she whispered as she bent closer to wipe away some more of the blood on his face. In a louder voice, she went on. "Some of these cuts ought to be stitched up, but I can't do that."

"It's all right," Fargo told her. "A few more scars won't matter."

Then he dropped his voice lower again and went on. "He can't do anything to us if we're well away from here before he knows we're gone."

"How would we manage that?"

Fargo thought about the sort of life that Slauson and Sharon had led before they double-crossed her husband. "Were you ever in on any of the swindles that Slauson and your husband pulled?"

She nodded. "Of course. We all worked together."

"Did you ever slip something into a man's drink to knock him out?"

Sharon's eyes widened as she saw what Fargo was getting at. "Yes," she said. "Yes, I did. And I still have some of the stuff." She paused. "But it's old . . . I don't know if it will still work."

"All you can do is try. If you can knock out Slauson and Julia and get me my guns, we'll get out of here. With some hard riding, we can be in Blackwater by morning."

"We could . . ." she said slowly, and Fargo knew she was considering the idea. Her blue eyes abruptly hardened with resolution. "I'll do it," she declared. "But what about Mac and Jimmy?"

"Leave them to me," Fargo said. "I'll knock them out somehow, then tie and gag them so none of the others will find them until morning. We'll slip away and be gone, and by the time the rest of them find out, it'll be too late to catch us."

Fargo hated like hell to be plotting against Julia this way, but he was convinced that she would never betray her father. She had said that she would try to help him escape, but in the end he didn't think she would go through with it.

Sharon would. Fargo was convinced of that.

But once Julia knew he had escaped, she would warn Slauson and tell him who Fargo really was. Slauson would probably be gone before Fargo could get back with the authorities.

Fargo had an idea how to deal with that, but he didn't say anything about it to Sharon, knowing that she would argue with him. He would wait until the time came, and she would have no choice but to go along with him.

"Give me an hour," he whispered. "The camp will pretty much be asleep by then, and that'll give you time to slip the stuff to Slauson and Julia. Be careful that they don't catch you."

"I will. You can be damned sure about that."

She straightened then as a footstep in the doorway warned them that Slauson was entering the cabin. "Do you think he'll live?" the boss outlaw asked mockingly.

Sharon straightened and tossed the bloody rag on the floor. "He'll be all right," she said. "Bruised and sore for a few days, but that's all."

"Have another drink with me, Smith?" Slauson asked as he swaggered over to the table.

Fargo shook his head. "No offense, Jack, but all I want to do is crawl in my blankets and get some rest. Fighting wears a man out."

"From what I hear, Rufe is still asleep," Slauson said with a chuckle. "Go ahead. Go back to your tent and take it easy."

"No guards?"

"Where can you go?" Slauson spread his hands. "We're in the middle of Death Valley."

Fargo stood up. "I'm glad I passed your little test," he said on his way out of the cabin.

"So am I," Slauson said. "If you hadn't, some of the boys would have to be digging a grave right about now."

9

Fargo found Mac and Jimmy smoking in front of the tent he shared with them. Mac had a pipe in his hand, Jimmy a quirly dangling from his lips.

"That was some tussle you had with Rufe," Jimmy said, the cigarette bobbing as he spoke. "I figured you'd get your head handed to you."

"Yeah, quite a fight," Mac agreed.

"You fellas aren't mad because I won?" Fargo asked.

Mac let out a snort. "To tell you the truth, Smith, Rufe is a damned bully. I reckon we all respect him, but you'll find that he doesn't have many real friends in the gang."

"Well, it's good to know that I won't have to worry too much about somebody trying to settle the score for him."

"Hell, no," Jimmy said. "We're glad you took him down a notch."

Mac pointed the stem of the pipe at Fargo. "When Rufe wakes up, now, you can worry about him. He won't like bein' beat that way."

"I'll worry about that when the time comes," Fargo said. "Right now I just want to get some rest."

Mac inclined his head toward the tent. "Go ahead. We'll be in directly."

Fargo ducked through the tent flap. It was dark

inside. He went to the back of the tent, thrust his hand under the canvas, and felt around outside until he found a fist-sized rock. He pulled it in.

Then he stretched out on his bedroll without crawling into it. He lay there quietly, keeping his breathing deep and regular even though he wasn't asleep. He could feel his muscles stiffening from the pounding that Rufe had given them and hoped it wouldn't be too long before Mac and Jimmy turned in. When the time came for action, he would have to move swiftly and surely.

Ten or fifteen minutes later the two outlaws came into the tent and lay down to sleep. Fargo waited. Minutes that seemed like hours dragged by. While he waited to be sure that Mac and Jimmy were asleep, he listened intently to the sounds that came from the rest of the camp. Quietness soon reigned.

Of course, there would be guards posted, but Fargo hoped to slip past them. He didn't plan to leave through the wash where the gang had come in, but rather he intended to follow the creek higher into the hills and circle around that way. The route would be longer but safer.

Finally satisfied that his companions were sound asleep, Fargo rolled onto his side and pushed himself to hands and knees. He listened to the sound of Mac's breathing and tried to judge exactly where the outlaw's head was. When he was satisfied, Fargo drew a deep breath and struck.

The rock thudded into Mac's head. Mac grunted in pain but didn't move. He wasn't just asleep now; he was unconscious and would stay that way for a good while. Long enough for Fargo's purposes, anyway.

The sound of the blow had intruded on Jimmy's sleep. The young owlhoot roused up, rolled over, and started to say, "Wha—"

Fargo swung the rock again, aiming at the sound of Jimmy's voice. The crashing impact knocked Jimmy flat on his back. He was out cold.

Fargo checked and found a pulse in both men. He hadn't killed them, and in a way he was glad of that, despite the fact that they were ruthless outlaws who no doubt had the blood of innocents on their hands many times over.

Jimmy had a knife sheathed on his belt. Fargo took it and used it to cut strips off one of the blankets. He used the strips to bind the two outlaws hand and foot, then cut off bigger pieces of the blanket for gags. Within minutes, Mac and Jimmy were trussed up and gagged so that they couldn't move or make a sound.

Fargo took their revolvers and tucked them behind his belt. He had told Sharon to get his weapons, but she might not be able to do that. At least this way he would be armed. He edged the tent flap aside and peered out at the outlaw camp.

It appeared to be sleeping in the moonlight. Fargo didn't see anyone moving around. He slipped out of the tent and turned toward the cabin.

The single window glowed with light. He cat-footed toward it, his hand on the butt of one of the guns, ready to snatch it out and blaze away if he needed to.

Of course, any shots would rouse the whole camp and probably sign his death warrant, so he didn't intend to use the gun unless he absolutely had to.

As he approached the cabin, he saw movement against the light. The door began to open. Tensing, Fargo went into a crouch. If Puma Jack Slauson stepped outside and saw him, the game was up and Colt flame would bloom in the night.

Instead, Sharon Bradley emerged from the cabin. Moonlight glinted on her glossy black hair.

"Sharon!" Fargo hissed.

She turned sharply toward him and said, "Thank God! I was just coming to look for you, Smith. Mac and Jimmy . . . ?"

"Out cold. They won't cause any trouble for us."

She came up to him and thrust a gun belt into his hands. "Here's your Colt. Jack had it." She took the Arkansas Toothpick, which was in its fringed sheath, from behind her belt. "And your knife. Your rifle is with your saddle, in the shed around back."

Fargo buckled on the gun belt, feeling the comforting weight of the Colt on his hip once more. He didn't take the time to strap the big knife to his leg but tucked it behind his belt instead as he hurried around the cabin with Sharon.

"There'll be a man guarding the horses," she whispered. "Can you take care of him quietly?"

"Get me close enough and I can."

They walked toward the corral. Even in the moonlight, Sharon's richly curved body made it obvious she was a woman. If the guard recognized her, he might assume that Fargo was Slauson. All Fargo needed was a moment's hesitation on the outlaw's part.

As they came closer and a man stepped out of the shadows carrying a rifle, Sharon called softly, "It's just us, Zeb."

The guard started to lower the rifle. "What's up, Jack?" he asked.

Fargo palmed out the Colt and struck as he stepped close to the man. The barrel thudded against the guard's head. The man's knees buckled. Fargo grabbed him and eased him to the ground.

"I'll get my Ovaro," he told Sharon. "You get two more horses and bring them over to the cabin so we can saddle them."

"Two?" Sharon repeated in surprise. "Why do we need a spare horse?"

"In case one goes lame," Fargo lied. If he told her what he really planned, she might balk.

Sharon seemed to accept the explanation. Talking quietly and soothingly to the horses, Fargo took down a couple of poles that served as a gate and went inside to get the Ovaro. He led the horse out while Sharon caught two more of the mounts. After closing the fence, they headed for the shed behind the cabin where all the saddles were kept.

Fargo got the stallion ready to ride and then left him there with the reins dangling. While Sharon was getting saddles on the other two mounts, Fargo hurried around the cabin to the door. He glanced over the camp, saw that it was still sleeping peacefully. He stepped inside.

Slauson sat at the table, his head down on the wooden surface as he snored softly. The knockout drops, or powder, or whatever it had been that Sharon had slipped to him, probably in a drink, had done the trick. Slauson didn't look like he would wake up for a long time.

But Fargo didn't see Julia. She didn't seem to be anywhere in the cabin. Fargo caught his breath. Something was wrong.

An instant later, he found out just how wrong, as Julia stepped out from behind the door and pressed the barrel of a gun against the back of Fargo's neck. "Don't move, Skye," she said. "I'd hate to have to shoot you after all we've been through."

Fargo stood stock-still, not wanting to spook her into pulling the trigger. "Take it easy, Julia," he said quietly.

"I was hoping that you weren't in on it with her. I was hoping you weren't trying to double-cross me."

"You've got that wrong," Fargo told her. "I was just—"

"I thought you were going to let me help you escape," Julia cut in, angry now. "Instead you've thrown in with *her*. That slut."

"If I'd played along with you, it would have just

gotten us both in trouble," Fargo said. "You couldn't ever turn on your father, Julia. I could see that. And even if I did get away, you'd warn him then and see to it that he left Death Valley."

"Of course I would have! I don't want the law to catch him. He'd hang, Skye."

Slauson deserved to hang, Fargo thought, but he didn't say that. He still hoped he could talk some sense into Julia, though he was beginning to doubt it.

"Just let us go," he said. "That way you're rid of Sharon and don't have to worry about her anymore."

"Once I tell my father what she did, I won't have to worry about her at all. Imagine trying to knock him out that way!"

"Looks like she succeeded," Fargo pointed out.

"Yes, but she failed with me," Julia said with some satisfaction. "I spotted what she was doing and just pretended to drink the coffee she fixed for us. Then I acted like I passed out, too, until she was gone. I wanted to see what she would do. I was hoping . . . I was really hoping you wouldn't show up, Skye."

She was close behind him, and Fargo knew he could probably jerk his head to the side, spin around, and knock the gun away from her without getting shot. She would have time to pull the trigger, though, and that shot would be his doom just as surely as if it hit him. He had to try something else, even if the chances weren't good . . .

"I hate to tell you this," he said, "but it looks like Sharon used too much of the stuff. I think your father has stopped breathing."

"What!" Julia exclaimed. The gun muzzle went away from Fargo's neck as she stepped to the side to peer around him at the table.

Fargo twisted and grabbed at the gun with his right hand. His fingers closed around the cylinder so that it couldn't turn. The pistol wouldn't fire even though Julia pulled on the trigger.

At the same time he continued pivoting toward her and struck with a loosely balled left fist. The punch caught her on the chin with enough force to rock her head back. Her eyes rolled up as the impact of the blow stunned her.

Fargo tore the gun out of her fingers and clapped his other hand over her mouth to keep her quiet. She was only half-conscious, though, and didn't try to yell or struggle as he hauled her out of the cabin and around to the back.

"Smith, what the hell!" Sharon said as she saw who Fargo had with him. "What are you doing with that little bitch?"

"The stuff didn't knock her out," Fargo replied truthfully. "She tried to stop me, so I had to clout her one."

That was better than admitting to Sharon that he had planned all along to bring Julia with them.

"Why didn't you just leave her there?" Sharon demanded. "You could have tied and gagged her, too."

"I thought about it, but I decided it might be better to take her with us, just in case Slauson gets on our trail too soon."

"You mean use her as a hostage?" Sharon sounded as if she liked that idea. "I suppose we could—"

"Good thing we've got an extra horse," Fargo hurried on, not letting Sharon have time to think too much about things. He pulled the tail of Julia's blouse out of her skirt, tore a piece off it, wadded up the cloth and stuck it in her mouth. He didn't take the time to tie it in place and make a proper gag of it, but he thought it would take her a while to spit it out.

Then he picked her up and slung her over the saddle on one of the horses. It took only a moment to lash her in place so she couldn't fall off.

She would be sick and sore when she woke up fully, Fargo thought, but that couldn't be helped. He took the reins of the stallion and the horse that was carrying Julia and started up the wash, following the creek toward the spring that fed it. Sharon came along behind him, leading her horse. They moved slowly and as quietly as possible.

The wash began climbing higher into the hills. Fargo paused, waited for Sharon to come up closer to him, and asked her, "Is there a guard up here?"

"Yes, but just one man. There are two on the other end."

"You know where he is?"

"Not really."

Fargo thought quickly. The guard would be more watchful for someone trying to sneak into the hideout, not out of it. He said, "We'll see if we can bluff him."

"If they come after us now . . ."

"I know," Fargo said. "We don't have a big enough lead yet. They'd catch us before we got across the salt flat."

"That's right. I can't ever go back, Smith. I've burned my bridges tonight."

"You won't have to go back," Fargo promised her. "Come on."

They followed the creek to the spring. Just as they got there, a voice called from a stand of scrubby trees, "Who's there?"

"It's Zeb," Fargo said roughly, remembering the name Sharon had spoken earlier. "Come to relieve you."

The sentry stepped out from the trees. "I ain't supposed to be relieved until mornin'."

"Puma Jack wants to see you." Fargo hoped that would be enough to draw the man a little closer. He slipped the Arkansas Toothpick out of its sheath.

"What the hell does Jack want—hey, you ain't Zeb! Who's that with—"

The guard didn't waste any more time on questions. He jerked his rifle up.

But at the same time, Fargo's arm went back, and before the outlaw could fire, Fargo's arm whipped forward and the big knife flew straight and true through the moonlight. The tip of the blade caught the guard in the throat. The Trailsman had put so much power behind the throw that the knife penetrated all the way through the man's neck and stuck out the back. With a hideous gurgle, the man dropped his rifle and pawed at the handle of the Toothpick.

When he pulled it free, a fountain of blood came with it, black in the moonlight instead of crimson as it sprayed down the front of his shirt. He collapsed and kicked a couple of times, then died with a rattling sigh.

Fargo picked up the knife and wiped the blade on the dead man's vest. "Let's go," he said icily. He couldn't afford to let himself feel anything at the moment. There would be time for emotions later . . . if they survived.

Though he was generally familiar with the landscape, he hadn't been in this part of Death Valley before and wasn't exactly sure where he was going. There were no trails to follow up here.

But his trailsman's instincts were unerring, and they found themselves in a corkscrew-shaped canyon that ran generally north. When they came out of it, they were on the edge of a wide salt flat.

Fargo thought he saw a light in the distance, far across the flats. That might be Blackwater, or it might be a prospectors' camp. Whichever, it was on the eastern side of Death Valley, and that was where Fargo wanted to go. The light would serve as a beacon to guide them across the flats.

There had been no signs of pursuit behind them. Now it was time for speed, not stealth. "Let me check on Julia," Fargo said to Sharon, "and then we'll mount up and light a shuck out of here."

"Why are you worried about her?" Sharon asked in a surly voice.

"I expected her to come around before now," Fargo explained. "I don't think I hit her hard enough to do any real damage, but I want to make sure."

"I'll see about her," Sharon said, moving toward the horse. "Men can't be trusted around that little Jezebel. She has ways of making them do anything she wants them to."

Fargo thought about objecting, but then he decided to let Sharon handle it. He swung up into the Ovaro's saddle instead.

A moment later he realized he had made a mistake. There were the sharp sounds of a scuffle in the darkness; then Sharon cried out, "Damn!"

Fargo wheeled the stallion and saw that Julia had gotten free somehow. She was on her feet, struggling with Sharon as the spooked horses plunged around them. Suddenly, the glow from the lowering moon glinted on the barrel of a gun in Julia's hand.

Sharon dived aside as Julia pulled the trigger. Screaming in rage, Julia thumbed off all the shots in the cylinder, and the thundering blasts rolled across the desolate landscape and echoed back from the gravelly hills.

The outlaw camp was only two or three miles away. The sound of the shots would travel that far easily in the thin air, Fargo knew.

The hammer of the pistol clicked on an empty chamber. Julia dropped the gun and turned to run. Blindly, she headed out onto the salt flats.

Fargo spurred after her and caught up to her in a matter of seconds. He leaned down from the saddle and wrapped an arm around her, plucking her up from the ground and throwing her across the saddle in front of him. He turned the Ovaro around and trotted back to where Sharon was brushing herself off after rolling on the ground.

"That bitch!" Sharon spat. "She tried to kill me!"

"Well, what did you try to do to me?" Julia demanded. "You poisoned my father!"

"The hell I did! I just gave him a few knockout drops. He won't even have much of a headache when he wakes up."

Fargo didn't want to waste any more time letting these two snipe at each other. He said, "What happened?"

"She got loose somehow," Sharon said. "I guess she'd been shamming most of the time since we left the camp."

Fargo frowned. "I tied those knots pretty good," he said.

Julia tossed her head angrily. "You thought you tied up a young woman who didn't know anything about getting loose," she said disdainfully. "I've been able to slip out of ropes like that for years, Skye."

"Skye!" Sharon exclaimed. "I thought your name was Chuckwalla Smith."

Fargo bit back a curse. There wasn't time for explanations. Those shots would have roused the camp, and the outlaws had probably found Slauson, Mac, and Jimmy by now. In a matter of minutes, they would be riding to investigate the flurry of gunfire.

"Mount up," he said to both women. "We've got to get across the flats."

"I'm not going anywhere with you," Julia snapped.

"If you don't, I'll hog-tie you good this time," Fargo warned. "Now get on that horse."

Julia hesitated, but then she put her foot in the stirrup and swung up into the saddle. "My father is going to kill you," she threatened.

"Maybe, but I'm not going to sit around and wait for him to do it."

Fargo took off his hat and slashed it across the rump of Julia's mount. The horse snorted and lunged forward into a gallop, heading farther out onto the salt flats.

Fargo and Sharon galloped after Julia. Fargo pointed out the distant light to Sharon and called, "Head for that spot!" If the light came from Blackwater, Slauson might not come all the way into the settlement after the fugitives. If it was a fire at some prospector's camp, maybe they could at least hole up there and try to hold off the outlaws.

The stallion could have outdistanced both of the other horses, but Fargo held him in, not allowing him to run full speed. If the outlaws caught up to them before they made it across the salt flats, he would have to fight a rear guard action.

They had a lead, but Fargo didn't know if it would be enough. The gang wouldn't have to follow the same roundabout route Fargo and his two companions had taken when they left the camp. The outlaws could ride straight toward the sound of the shots.

Then it would be a matter of whether or not they could pick up the trail. The hooves of the stallion and the other two horses left pretty visible tracks in the dry crust that lay over the vast expanse of salt.

It was about ten miles straight across the flats. Fargo checked their back trail frequently, and he estimated they had covered about half that distance when he spotted a large, dark shape moving over the flats behind them.

That shape was a tightly packed group of riders. Fargo was certain of it. The outlaws were on their trail. He didn't know if the owlhoots had been able to rouse Slauson, but even if Puma Jack wasn't with them, they would ride hard to catch up to their quarry. None of the men would want to disappoint their feared leader.

"Go!" Fargo shouted to the two women.

Sharon urged her horse on, but Julia began to drop

back. Fargo figured she was slowing down on purpose, trying to give the outlaws a better chance to catch them. As he drew even with her, he swerved toward her, reaching out to grab the reins from her.

But even as he did so, he noticed the hitch in the horse's gait. The animal had gone lame. No amount of prodding would make it run any faster than it was now. In fact, if the horse didn't slow down even more, the leg might give out completely and it wouldn't even be able to walk.

Fargo dropped the reins and leaned over to take hold of Julia instead. She cried out in surprise as he pulled her out of the saddle. He lifted her in front of him, sliding back a little to make more room for her on the Ovaro's back. Without a rider, the other horse started walking and quickly fell behind them.

"Hang on," Fargo told Julia. The magnificent stallion had barely broken stride when the extra weight landed on his back. He was still running fast and easy across the salt flat.

But even the Ovaro had his limits. Carrying double like this at a gallop would tax his reserves of strength. Fargo knew his horse well, and he hoped the stallion had enough stamina to get them across the flats.

Sharon's horse had pulled ahead. With the added weight, the Ovaro couldn't catch up completely, but he cut the gap a little. The hills on the far side of the flats were distinctly visible in the moonlight but seemed to be drawing no closer. Fargo knew that was an illusion. They were getting there. Just a little longer . . .

He glanced back and saw that the outlaws were closer, too, probably no more than half a mile behind them.

Julia turned her head and shouted over the rush of the wind and the thunder of hooves, "Why don't you let me go? I'll make them turn back!"

She wouldn't be able to make the gang give up the chase, Fargo thought, and she probably knew that, too. At best, she would slow them down for a moment while they picked her up. Then they would be right back on the trail, and even worse, they would have no reason not to fire indiscriminately at the fugitives. The owlhoots would probably be shooting already if not for the fact that they were scared of hitting their leader's daughter.

"Skye, listen to me! You can't get away!"

"We'll see about that," Fargo gritted. He thought the hills looked a little closer now . . .

Close enough, in fact, that he was able to pick out some familiar shapes. He realized they were riding toward the canyon where a few days earlier he and Julia had encountered Gypsum Dailey and Frank Jordan. That light up ahead was a campfire a short distance inside the canyon mouth, he guessed.

As they drew nearer, a muzzle flash winked in the night up ahead. Fargo heard the whine of the bullet passing overhead and knew it had been a warning shot.

"Hold your fire!" he bellowed. "Jordan! Dailey! It's me, Fargo!"

There were no more shots. A few moments later, Fargo and Sharon reined in as they came up to the fire. The old tent, ragged now from being trampled, had been set up again. Gypsum and Jordan emerged from behind some rocks as the three riders hastily dismounted, and to Fargo's surprise he saw there was a third man with them.

"That really you, Fargo?" this third man asked, and the Trailsman recognized the voice.

"Hello, Chuckwalla," Fargo said as he slid his Henry out of the saddle boot and faced back toward the canyon mouth.

"Wait a minute!" Sharon exclaimed. "This old man is really Chuckwalla Smith?"

"Who you callin' old, gal?" the bearded prospector demanded.

"Then who are you?" Sharon asked Fargo. "I know she called you Skye, and then . . . wait a minute. Fargo? Skye Fargo? You are the Trailsman."

Fargo grunted. "Guilty as charged." He could hear the rolling thunder of the gang's horses approaching. He said to Gypsum, Jordan, and Chuckwalla, "Boys, there are more than two dozen outlaws chasing us. Are you up to a fight?"

"Puma Jack's bunch?" Jordan asked.

"That's right."

"Damn right we'll fight 'em," Gypsum rumbled. "Sorry, ladies, didn't mean to cuss."

"Who're you?" Chuckwalla asked Sharon. "You ain't Puma Jack's woman, are you?"

"Not anymore," she replied.

The old pelican looked from Sharon to Julia. "And you're the gal who was lookin' for her pa."

"She found him," Fargo said. "He's Puma Jack."

That flabbergasted the three prospectors even more, but explanations could wait until later. Fargo waved them toward the canyon mouth, where there were several boulders that would provide cover.

"I'm going with you," Sharon said as she drew the gun at her hip. "I can shoot as good or better than most of those men."

Fargo thought about it for a second, then nodded. Sharon had a big stake in this, too. She had betrayed Slauson, and he had no doubt the man would kill her if he got his hands on her. She had a right to be in on this battle.

He glanced at Julia, not knowing what to expect from her.

"I'm staying out of it," she said in answer to his unspoken question. "You can't expect me to shoot at my own father."

"Can we trust you at our backs, or do I need to tie you up?" he asked tautly.

"I said I was staying out of it. I meant it."

Fargo still wasn't sure whether to believe her, but his instincts told him she was telling the truth.

"Let's go," he snapped as he led the small force of defenders forward to take up their positions. There were only five of them, which meant the odds were more than five to one. They had decent cover, though, while the outlaws were out in the open.

One way or another, the battle was about to be joined.

10

Fargo put Gypsum, Jordan, and Chuckwalla behind some rocks on the right side of the canyon mouth while he and Sharon took up their position behind a large boulder on the left. The moon was about to set behind the Panamints. Once it did, the night would be stygian for a time before the sky began to lighten with the approach of dawn.

"If Slauson is smart, he'll wait a little while," Fargo commented. "We can still see pretty well right now, and we can lay down good fire over that open ground in front of us."

"Jack is smart, all right," Sharon said. "He was a fine officer when he was in the army, from what I've heard."

Fargo glanced over at her. "What made him go bad again?"

She shrugged and said, "Who knows? He came from a life of crime on the Trace, seemed to put it behind him, then went back to being a swindler and an outlaw and a killer. Maybe being honest was just too damned hard for him. I know it was that way for my husband."

"You thought it would be different when you went with Slauson?"

Sharon laughed humorlessly. "What I thought doesn't matter a hoot in hell. I was tired of Will, and he was mean to me sometimes, too. Jack's older, but he's still a handsome man." She paused and then added, "What I didn't know was that he can be an even bigger bastard than Will ever was."

"He beat you?" Fargo asked quietly.

"No." Sharon's voice was hollow, and Fargo didn't know if she was going to go on or not, but after a moment she said, "He let some of the other men bed me while he watched. It was like a reward for doing their job when they pulled a robbery. I guess he figured I was already a slut, so it didn't matter."

Fargo's face was grim. He already figured that Slauson deserved a bullet or a hang rope, and what he had just heard sure didn't change his opinion any.

"Here they come!" Chuckwalla whooped from the other side of the canyon mouth.

Fargo saw the riders charging the canyon in the moonlight. The outlaws began to fire. Slauson might still be worried about a stray bullet hitting Julia, but there was no way for the outlaws to get into the canyon without fighting their way in.

"Let 'em have it!" Fargo shouted. He brought the Henry to his shoulder and began to fire as fast as he could work the rifle's lever.

He poured lead into the dark mass that was the charging outlaws. Close beside him, Sharon's pistol blasted. The cracking of rifles came from the other side of the canyon mouth, punctuated by the dull boom of Gypsum's shotgun.

Through the drifting gun smoke, Fargo saw the front ranks of the attackers shatter and break apart under the withering volley. The outlaws couldn't aim very well from their saddles, so most of their bullets went wild. A few of them came close enough to splatter on the boulder or whine off in a ricochet, but they didn't do any real damage.

As the riders peeled away, leaving two of their number sprawled motionless on the ground, Fargo saw that the whole gang hadn't taken part in the charge. Only eight of the outlaws had galloped toward the canyon, whooping and firing as they came.

The attack had been nothing but a preliminary thrust, Fargo realized. Slauson had risked those men solely to judge the strength of the defenders. Now he knew that there were five guns facing him, and that the cover inside the canyon mouth was good.

Slauson wouldn't waste any more men on a direct attack. Fargo was sure of that. Instead he would wait until after the moon had set and try something else.

"That didn't amount to much," Sharon said as she took fresh cartridges from the loops on her belt and thumbed them into the revolver's empty chambers.

"It wasn't meant to." Quickly, Fargo explained his theory.

"I'm afraid you're right," she agreed. "Jack is too canny a leader to throw away his men's lives for nothing."

Fargo finished reloading the Henry. "Why is he called Jack when his name is Arthur?" he asked idly.

"I have no idea. Like I told you, he got the name while he was growing up on the Natchez Trace. I suppose one of the other cutthroats gave it to him for some reason."

"As dangerous as a puma, maybe," Fargo mused.

"I wouldn't doubt it."

From the other side of the canyon mouth, Chuckwalla called across, "Everybody all right over there, Fargo?"

"Fine," Fargo answered. "How about you boys?"

"Nary a scratch!"

They would be mighty lucky if they could still say that by the time the sun rose, Fargo thought.

The moon dropped behind the mountains a short time later, its departure casting a nigh-impenetrable pall over the rugged landscape, without the gang making any further attempts to take the canyon.

In less than an hour, the sky would begin to turn gray as dawn approached. Until then, though, Slauson's men could work their way closer to the canyon without the defenders being able to see them. It was also possible that they might try to climb into the hills on either side of the canyon so that they could fire down into it.

Leaving the others at the canyon mouth for a few minutes, Fargo hurried back to the prospectors' camp and called Julia's name. She crawled out of the tent.

"I didn't think they would mind," she said, gesturing toward the shelter. "I laid low in there while the shooting was going on."

"That was a good idea," Fargo said with a nod, "but you need to move even farther back now. Just keep going and follow the canyon for a half-mile or so. That'll put you out of danger."

"My father is going to kill all of you, you know," she said softly. "I don't care about Sharon, but you and those three prospectors . . . none of you deserve to die, Skye."

"The gang has already been wiping out prospectors, remember?" Fargo pointed out. "You know your father wants to run everyone out of Death Valley and kill the ones who won't leave."

"He just wants someplace where he and his men can be safe—"

"Safe from the law," Fargo interrupted her. "Safe from justice."

She came closer to him, put her arms around him, rested her head against his chest. "I know," she whispered. "I can't argue with you, Skye. But he's my father. And I've been a criminal, too. I'm just as bad as the rest of them."

"If you really believed that, it wouldn't be tearing you up inside."

"That's what life does," she said. "It confuses you and pulls you first one way and then the other, and in the end all you can do is pray you've followed the right trail." She tipped her head back and looked up into his face. "You're the Trailsman . . . you should know about that."

Fargo didn't know what to say to that. He brushed his lips across hers in a kiss, then said, "Get on up the canyon. Don't come back until it's light and you can see what's going on. You should be safe."

"Nobody is really safe," she said, and then she was gone.

Fargo went back to the rocks at the mouth of the canyon and asked Sharon, "Any sign of them?"

She shook her head. "Nothing. But I know they're still out there." She hesitated. "Did you send her away?"

"Yes."

"Good. It's not really her fight. Nobody gets to choose their family."

Fargo was surprised to hear her speaking like that about Julia. "She ought to be all right, no matter how things turn out. Slauson can't hold her responsible for anything that's happened."

"I don't know about that. She brought *you* to Death Valley."

That was true enough, Fargo supposed. But he still didn't think Slauson would take any revenge on Julia.

He didn't say anything else but concentrated on listening instead. Since even his keen eyes weren't much good in this darkness, he had to rely on his ears.

Fortunately, his hearing was above average, too, so he caught the faint whisper of boot leather on sand coming from close by and knew hell was about to pop again.

Fargo twisted toward the sound and brought the rifle up just as several of the outlaws charged in

146

among the rocks. They must have crawled up close before leaping to their feet and lunging forward. Gun flashes threw a hellish flickering light over the scene as the owlhoots opened fire.

Fargo heard the wind-rip of bullets close by his ear as he returned the fire. Rock splinters stung his cheek as slugs smacked into the boulder beside him. The Henry was like a thing alive as it blasted and bucked in his hands. He caught glimpses of men spinning off their feet and heard the boom of the shotgun and deep-throated yells from Gypsum as the burly prospector joined the fight on the other side of the canyon.

A rattle of gravel made Fargo spin even more. "Behind us!" he shouted. More of the outlaws had circled up into the hills and were trying to bushwhack them. A few yards from Fargo, Sharon's pistol blasted a steady stream of lead until she suddenly cried out in pain.

Fargo figured she was hit but had no time to find out how badly she was hurt. He had emptied all fifteen shots in the Henry and was still under attack. He spotted one of the outlaws charging him, a deeper blotch of shadow moving through other shadows.

As a gun thundered practically right in his face, Fargo dove to the ground and thrust out the barrel of the rifle. The attacker tripped over it and tumbled off his feet, cursing as he fell. Those curses served as a guide for Fargo as he came up on his knees and drove the Henry's brass-plated buttstock into the middle of the man's face. He felt as much as heard the bones crunch and shatter.

Rolling over, Fargo dropped the empty rifle and drew his Colt as he came to his feet. The shooting seemed to have stopped, though, and he heard only one person breathing harshly near him.

"Sharon?" he said, knowing that he risked giving his position away.

"Yeah . . . I'm hit, Smith . . . I mean, Fargo." She

gave a hollow laugh. "I can't get used to calling you that."

He moved over beside her and dropped to a knee. "How bad is it?"

"Don't know. I was hit in the side . . . there's a lot of blood, and I'm starting to feel cold."

"It's cold out here," Fargo said as he reached out to touch her and felt the wet warmth on her side. "But it'll be morning soon."

"Not . . . soon enough."

"Hang on," he urged her. "Just hang on."

That was all he could do. He couldn't strike a light to tend to her wound. He didn't think Slauson would give him a chance to do that, anyway. The defenders had beaten off another attack, but Slauson wouldn't let up on the pressure. Fargo was sure there would be yet another round within minutes.

He was right. This time, the outlaws came on horseback again. Fargo had no idea how Gypsum, Jordan, and Chuckwalla had fared during the previous fracas, but as hooves pounded and guns began to roar again, he heard both rifles and the shotgun join the fray from the other side of the canyon mouth. All three of the prospectors were at least in good enough shape to pull the trigger.

Fargo emptied his Colt at the riders who galloped past, firing to right and left as they came. A bullet tugged at the sleeve of his shirt and another knocked his hat off his head, but that was as close as they came.

Some of the outlaws made it into the canyon, though, and charged on up a short distance before wheeling their horses. Fargo bit back a curse. He had been worried about just this possibility. He and his friends were caught between two fires now. They had dealt out some serious damage to Slauson's forces, he thought, but they were still outnumbered, and now Slauson could pinch them from both sides.

148

Fargo barely had time to catch his breath and thumb fresh cartridges into the revolver before more shooting erupted. The gunfire came from outside the canyon, but after a second, he realized there was something different about it. The shots didn't seem to be directed toward the canyon.

It sounded almost like the outlaws were fighting among themselves.

But that didn't make any sense, and Fargo didn't have time to puzzle it out. The members of the gang who had made it into the canyon were attacking again, charging back toward the boulders that shielded the defenders.

Fargo bellied down on the rocky ground as a curtain of lead ripped through the air above him. He realized he could *see* the outlaws now as they charged him. Dawn was closer than he had thought. He aimed carefully but quickly, drawing a bead, squeezing the trigger, and then shifting the Colt before the first man he had shot tumbled from the saddle. Fargo had filled all six chambers in the cylinder, and he emptied all six in a matter of seconds.

But he emptied four saddles, too, and withering fire from the other side of the canyon mouth blew the remaining three outlaws to hell.

The expected attack from outside had never materialized. Fargo came up on his knees and swiftly reloaded, just in case. He heard more riders galloping toward the canyon and swung around in a crouch, ready to meet the threat.

The men didn't come shooting, though. A voice yelled harshly, "Hold your fire! Hold your fire!" Fargo recognized it.

Slauson.

The son of a bitch had his nerve, Fargo thought, asking them not to shoot as he rode into the canyon. But he held his finger off the trigger anyway, just to see what was going to happen.

Four riders swept past the boulders and reined in. In the graying light, Fargo saw that one of the men was Slauson. Were the other three outlaws the only members of the gang left?

"Hold it, Slauson!" Fargo called as the boss outlaw dismounted. Fargo leveled the Colt at him. "Drop your guns!"

"Don't be a damned fool!" Slauson snapped. "We were bushwhacked out there. Between you and whoever it was that jumped us, nearly all my men are dead. We've got to call a truce and fight together, Smith!"

"The name is Fargo," the Trailsman said coolly. "And why should we fight on your side now?"

"To save your own hides, damn it! They'll kill you, too!"

"Will Bradley and the gunmen he hired to track you down don't have any grudge against me and my friends," Fargo said, making an educated guess as to the identities of the strangers who had joined the battle. "In fact, if we turn over you and your men, Bradley might be grateful enough to let us go in peace."

The sky was light enough now for Fargo to see the way Slauson's face contorted in rage. "Damn you!" he shouted. "I'll kill you if it's the last thing I do!"

His hand stabbed toward the gun on his hip.

Fargo was already holding his Colt. Slauson wouldn't have had a chance, even if Fargo had fired. But before he could tip up the revolver's barrel and squeeze the trigger, a shot blasted from somewhere on his right. Slauson cried out and rocked back a step. His gun was only halfway out of its holster. He tried again to draw it, and again a shot roared.

The bullet kicked Slauson backward. He caught himself, fell to his knees, and stared toward the boulder where Sharon sat propped up against the rock, a smoking gun in her hands. She had to use both of them to hold the weapon up.

"Sharon!" Slauson croaked.

She shot him again, this time hitting him in the center of the forehead. A black hole appeared there as the bullet bored on through his brain and blasted out the back of his skull. Slauson went over backward, twitching as he died.

Fargo had the other three outlaws covered, as did Chuckwalla, Gypsum, and Jordan, who came limping out of the boulders on the other side of the canyon. All three of the prospectors were wounded, Fargo saw, but they seemed to be moving fairly well.

One of the remaining owlhoots was Mac. He unbuckled his gun belt and let it fall at his feet. "Don't shoot," he said as he raised his hands. The other two men followed suit. "It's over," Mac said. "We don't want no more trouble."

"Keep an eye on them," Fargo said to Chuckwalla, who nodded grimly. Fargo swung around and hurried over to the boulder where Sharon sat.

Her buckskin shirt was dark with blood in the gray light. She coughed as Fargo knelt beside her, and more blood trickled from her mouth.

"Told you . . . I was hit too bad to make it," she gasped out. "But I lasted . . . long enough . . . to get old Puma Jack . . ."

"He's dead, all right," Fargo told her. "But you still need to hang on. I think your husband's out there. He jumped into the fight on our side."

"He's not . . . on your side . . . Watch him, Smith . . . I mean . . . oh, hell . . . He'll kill you, too . . . if he gets . . . gets the chance—"

Sharon's head lolled back against the rock. The life went out of her eyes.

Fargo knelt there beside her for a long moment before he sighed and looked up at the sky above the Funeral Mountains to the east. It was rosy now.

The sun would be up soon.

Mac had said it was over, but maybe it was and maybe it wasn't. Fargo gently closed Sharon's lifeless eyes and then stood up.

He walked over to the three prisoners and asked, "What happened out there?"

"A bunch of gun-throwers jumped us from behind," Mac replied. "We never saw 'em coming. They blasted the hell out of us. When there were only a few of us left, Puma Jack yelled for us to hightail it in here."

"You know who those men are and why they attacked you?"

"Mr. Whoever-the-Hell-You-Are, I don't know and I don't care," Mac said bitterly. "I figure we're all damned anyway."

"How many were there?"

"Hard to tell in the dark. Half a dozen, maybe more. We prob'ly outnumbered them at first, but they hit us so hard when we weren't expecting it that they evened up the odds in a hurry."

Fargo nodded. He was convinced that the bushwhackers worked for Will Bradley. They had gotten on Julia's trail in Los Angeles, and in the end she had led them to her father. Fargo still suspected that was what Bradley had had in mind all along.

Whether or not Bradley himself was out there with them was a question he couldn't answer. Sharon had seemed to think it was likely, or she wouldn't have warned Fargo against trusting him.

At the moment, Fargo wasn't in much of a mood to trust anybody.

So far, the strangers hadn't tried to attack the canyon. Now, as the sun began to peek over the mountains to the east, a man called from outside, "Hello in there! Anybody alive?"

"We're alive!" Fargo shouted back without identifying who he was or how many men were with him. "Who are you, and what do you want?"

"My name is William Bradley," the voice came back, confirming Fargo's guess. "I want Arthur Slauson and my wife, Sharon Bradley. Give them to me, and I'll let the rest of you go."

Fargo's instincts told him Bradley was lying. Sharon had been right to warn him about her husband. But there was a way of finding out.

"Slauson is dead!" Fargo called. "So is your wife! I'm sorry, Bradley!"

For a long moment, there was silence. Then Bradley asked, "What happened?"

"Sharon killed Slauson, then died from wounds she received in the fighting earlier. Slauson was trying to kill all of us, including her."

"She turned on him?" Bradley laughed loudly, and it was an ugly sound. "How fitting that they killed each other. They deserved such a fate."

Fargo didn't say anything.

"What about pretty little Julia?" Bradley asked. "She must be out here somewhere."

"I don't know anything about her," Fargo said. "Don't know where she is."

"You're lying, mister," Bradley shot back. "I've got a hunch you're the man who brought her out here. I'm a little disappointed not to get my hands on Slauson and his whore, but if you give me Julia, the rest of you can ride away from here. I've no quarrel with you."

Fargo remembered what Sharon had said about Bradley's cruelty. If the man couldn't have his revenge on his former partner and his wife, he was willing to settle for his partner's daughter. Fargo didn't know what hellish plans Bradley might have for Julia, but he wasn't just going to turn her over to him.

He was about to say as much when she spoke up from behind him. "Let me go, Skye," she said. "Maybe he'll leave the rest of you alone."

Fargo turned his head to look at her. He hadn't noticed her coming from farther up the canyon because he had been concentrating on the exchange with Bradley.

"I told you to stay back where it's safe," he said.

"I came out when the shooting was over." She glanced toward her father's bloody, sprawled form, and Fargo saw the pain in her eyes. Despite everything Slauson had done, Julia mourned him anyway. Some bonds could never be broken.

"Go on back," Fargo said gently.

Julia shook her head. "I know Will. I can persuade him to let the rest of you go."

"And what will he do to you if he gets his hands on you?"

Her chin came up. "I don't care. Some of . . . all this . . . is my fault. If I hadn't come running out here to Death Valley . . . if I hadn't gotten you and everyone else involved in Will's vendetta . . ."

Frank Jordan spoke up. "There's an old saying, miss, about how if wishes were horses, beggars might ride. I take that to mean that there's no use in worrying about what might have been."

"You should listen to Frank, ma'am," Gypsum put in. "He's a mighty smart man."

"That's right," Chuckwalla added. "I figured that out mighty fast, and all I did was spend a night with these boys on my way back from Blackwater."

"Miss Julia," Mac said, "if this hombre here"—he gestured toward Fargo —"will let us have our guns back, we'll fight for you, sure enough. Won't we, boys?"

The other two outlaws nodded and muttered their agreement.

Julia looked at Fargo and asked, "What do you think, Skye?"

Before Fargo could answer, Will Bradley called from outside the canyon, "I'm tired of waiting! We're coming in, and if Julia Slauson is there, we're taking her!"

Fargo nodded at Mac and the other outlaws. "Pick up your guns, men. The ball's back on."

They grabbed their weapons and scattered, spreading out among the rocks. Fargo didn't know how many hired guns Bradley had, but from what Mac had said, the odds would be pretty even this time. Julia was armed as well, and Fargo knew she wouldn't hesitate to use the pistol in her hand.

He took her with him and crouched behind a different boulder from the one where Sharon's body lay, though he could still see her from the corner of his eye. As he heard the steady clip-clop of hoofbeats, Fargo eased his head around the big rock to take a look. He saw two men riding into the mouth of the canyon. One was a roughly dressed, hard-faced gunman.

The other was younger and wore a town suit, though it was covered with trail dust at the moment. He was lean and handsome, with his black hat shoved back on his head, revealing thick, dark, curly hair. Even at this distance, Fargo could see the arrogance on his face. He knew he was looking at Will Bradley.

"Last chance," Bradley called as he reined in. "Give me Julia."

Fargo looked over at her and nodded. She flashed him a brief smile, then shouted in a loud, clear voice, "Go to hell, Will!"

Bradley's face twisted in anger. He jerked a gun from a holster on his hip and spurred forward, shooting as he came.

Fargo drew a bead on Bradley and was ready to calmly blast him out of the saddle, but before he could pull the trigger a bullet whipped over his shoulder and smacked into the boulder beside his head, spraying rock dust in his eyes. As Fargo blinked rapidly, trying to clear his vision, he heard more shots coming from above and behind them.

Bradley had taken a trick out of Slauson's repertoire and sent some of his gunmen into the hills above the canyon. Fargo twisted and rolled onto his back, bringing up the Colt. He spotted a man darting along a ledge and pulled the trigger. The revolver bucked against his hand as it roared. The gunman folded up in the middle and pitched forward off the ledge, bouncing off the canyon wall a couple of times before he landed in a heap on the ground.

The thunder of gunshots filled the canyon and echoed back from its walls. Fargo picked off another of the bushwhackers. He rolled again as Bradley and the other horsebacker galloped past. Bradley twisted in the saddle and fired. The bullet burned along the outside of Fargo's upper left arm. He gritted his teeth against the pain and squeezed off another shot, but Bradley jerked his horse to the side at that moment and Fargo's bullet missed.

Chuckwalla went down as a bullet knocked a chunk of meat off his thigh. Gypsum lunged out from behind a rock and tackled the other gunman on horseback, pulling him down from the saddle and throwing his arms around him in a bone-crushing, backbreaking bear hug. Frank Jordan fired at the men on the rocks above the canyon, as did Mac and the other two outlaws. One of the owlhoots staggered back and fell, the front of his shirt turning red with blood.

Fargo scrambled to his feet. It was hard to see through the clouds of gun smoke that filled the canyon, but he saw Mac go down, falling to his knees but still firing, not letting go of his gun until he pitched forward on his face. The third outlaw was wounded, too, and pulled himself up for one final shot before collapsing.

But the bushwhackers were falling, too, and after

a moment only one man seemed to be firing from the hillside. Chuckwalla had pulled himself into a sitting position and reloaded his old single-shot rifle. He blazed away just as Jordan fired again, and the last of Bradley's hired guns rolled out from behind the rock where he had been crouched, drilled cleanly through the head and chest.

That left just Will Bradley, and with an incoherent cry of rage, he spurred toward Fargo and Julia. Fargo stood up and tried to thrust Julia behind him with his wounded arm, but she slipped away. She stood beside him and lifted her gun.

She and Fargo both fired at the same time. So did Bradley.

Bradley's bullet went between them and splattered off the rock behind them. But the slugs fired by Fargo and Julia drove into Bradley's chest and smashed him back off the horse, flinging him out of the saddle like a giant hand had swatted him. He landed on his back and skidded a few inches over the sandy canyon floor, then came to a stop with his arms and legs outflung. His chest rose once as he gasped in a final breath, then fell and didn't rise again.

"You're hurt, Skye," Julia said as she clutched his arm.

"I'll live," Fargo assured her.

That was more than the dozens of bodies scattered around the canyon could claim. Fargo had to wonder if Death Valley had ever witnessed such a scene of carnage before.

This morning, at least, the place sure as hell had lived up to its name.

Mac and the other two outlaws who had joined forces with the canyon's defenders at the last were all dead. Fargo dug graves for them, along with one for Sharon.

The bodies of Slauson, Bradley, and the rest of the

slain outlaws and gunmen went into a ravine up in the hills. Fargo used his shovel to dig around a loose slope of gravel until it collapsed, slid down into the ravine, and covered the corpses.

His left arm was stiff and sore from the bullet burn, but he cleaned the minor wound and bound it up and knew he would be fine. Chuckwalla, Gypsum, and Frank Jordan all had assorted creases and flesh wounds. Julia was kept busy that morning tending to the prospectors' injuries.

By the middle of the day, though, she and Fargo were ready to ride for Blackwater. Fargo had been up to the spring at the head of the canyon and filled their canteens.

"You boys can do your prospecting in peace," Fargo told the men as he and Julia mounted their horses. "Nobody will bother you now."

"Thanks to you, Fargo," Chuckwalla said as he leaned on his rifle and used it as a makeshift crutch.

Fargo shook his head. He didn't want any credit for cleaning up Slauson's gang. "That's just the way things worked out," he said. He lifted a hand in farewell as he wheeled the Ovaro and headed north. Julia fell in alongside him.

"What about my wagon?" she asked as they rode.

"It's still at Furnace Creek. I reckon you can find some men in Blackwater to go down there and bring it back for you."

"There are a bunch of horses running loose, too," she said, referring to the mounts that had belonged to the outlaws and to Will Bradley's men. "I was thinking that I might try to round them up, sell them, and give the money to Chuckwalla and Frank and Gypsum." She hesitated for a second. "I could use some help with all that, Skye."

Fargo shook his head. "Not me. I'm ready to move on."

"I think I understand. Once I'm done here, I never want to see Death Valley again."

Fargo didn't say anything. He was sure that at some point down the path, the trails he followed would bring him back to this harsh, desolate, yet oddly beautiful land.

But not anytime soon. Right now he was anxious to see the high country again, to take a deep breath of clean mountain air, and to listen to the music of a cold, fast-flowing stream filled with nice fat trout. A few weeks of that would clear out all the bad memories that might otherwise linger.

"You can at least say a proper good-bye to me before you go, can't you?" Julia asked, almost as if she had read his mind.

As he thought about her smooth, supple body and all the delights it held, Fargo smiled.

Those trout could wait a few more days for him to get there, he reckoned.

LOOKING FORWARD!
**The following is the opening
section from the next novel in the
exciting *Trailsman* series from Signet:**

THE TRAILSMAN #280

TEXAS TART

*Texas, 1861. A stolen fortune, a prison where the
guards are more dangerous than the inmates,
and a beautiful woman more dangerous than both.*

The man with the lake-blue eyes sat his Ovaro stallion and stared down the slope at the campfire. A
lone man squatted there, drinking coffee from a tin
cup.

The time was near midnight on a lonely stretch of
Texas prairie where, if you were lucky, you spotted
a few adobe huts from time to time, and maybe a
corral or two made of ocotillo canes. A man had to
be hardy to live here. The local Indians were peace-
ful, but not the wandering war parties of the Apaches.
They didn't like Mexicans any more than they liked
whites.

The quarter moon helped hide the Trailsman and his Ovaro behind a copse of jack pines. The moon was pale and ragged gray rain clouds dragged across it. While this was the land where cattle was king, this section of the Rio Grande valley produced rich quantities of onions, spinach, carrots, and many fruits as well.

Skye Fargo was a man of experience. Take campfires—inviting as they always looked to a saddle-weary soul like Fargo—you could never be sure what you were getting into.

Fargo touched his holstered Colt as if for luck, and kneed his horse down the grassy slope toward the fire. Hot coffee would taste mighty good on a chill April night.

Hearing Fargo approach, the campfire man stood up and peered into the darkness. "And who would that be?" he said, his right hand dropping to his own gun.

"Somebody who'd appreciate a little bit of fire and a cup of coffee."

"You mind puttin' your hands up when you come into the campsite here?"

Fargo laughed. "Been on this horse so long, I could use the exercise."

The man's caution was reassuring. He was as leery of Fargo as Fargo was of him.

Fargo, his face now painted with the red and gold of the campfire, eased himself into the small circle where the man had set his saddle, his saddlebags, and his rife. He held a Navy Colt.

"Sorry to be so suspicious," the man said.

He was tall, angular, with a sharply boned face and nervous dark eyes. He huddled deep inside his sheepskin.

Fargo climbed down from the stallion.

The man walked over and offered his hand. "Curtis Devol. Was a ranch hand till yesterday." He smiled. "Got a little too drunk in town the night before. Guess I told the boss what I thought of him. Guess it wasn't too pretty." He nodded to the fire. "Help yourself to the coffee. There're a couple biscuits left, too."

"Obliged. My name's Fargo, by the way. Skye Fargo."

Devol's eyes narrowed. "That name's familiar somehow." He shrugged. "Coffee's all yours, mister."

Fargo went back to his horse and dragged out his own tin cup. He haunched down to pick up the coffeepot. "So where you headed now?"

Devol stood above him on the other side of the fire. "Driftin', I guess. Don't have a skill or a trade. Wish I did. My brother's a blacksmith over to Abilene. Makes himself a right nice bit of money."

Devol wasn't kidding about lacking a skill—at least as an actor. The way his gaze suddenly flicked to the right, the way his jaws bulged in apprehension, the way his body gave an involuntary start— Fargo didn't know what to expect for sure but he had a pretty good idea. He spun around on his haunches, hurled the coffeepot and its scalding contents up into the face of the man behind him, and then jerked to his feet, filling his hand with his Colt and blasting the revolver from Curtis Devol's gun hand.

The coffee-drenched man screamed and covered his face with his hands. Fargo stepped over to him and yanked the revolver from his hand, pitching it far into the shallow woods to the east. Fargo could see that the coffee had left the other man's face welted and violently scalded.

Devol was favoring his hand.

"Take your friend down to the creek there," Fargo

said to Devol. "Let him soak his face in the water for a while."

He walked back to his Ovaro and mounted up. "I ever see either of you again, you're dead. You would've robbed me and killed me tonight and that ain't anything I'm likely to forget."

He rode back up the slope and disappeared into the night. He could hear the scalded man's sobs for a long time.

The town of Cross Peak was named because of the way two angled rock outcroppings looked like crossed swords when approached from the northeast. It was a shopping hub and railroad dispatch center for this part of Texas. The mayor, who had been an Easterner until six years ago, had decided to show these hicks how to build a civilized town. And damned if his intentions weren't impressive to look at.

Fargo couldn't recall ever seeing such a clean city. Three long blocks of stores, all kept freshly painted with board sidewalks running in the front and carefully raked streets dividing west side from east side. The people seemed friendlier here, too, as if the mayor had mandated that along with his orders about keeping everything clean and orderly.

The town was so friendly, in fact, that each of the four hotels had attractive young women standing at the entrances and beckoning Fargo to come over. He passed up the chance to meet the first three women but the fourth, a brunette in a yellow cotton dress that made her look downright festive, just couldn't be passed by.

He hauled his saddlebags up to the girl. "This town is so friendly, a fella could get downright suspicious."

She laughed, throwing her head back and revealing a long elegant neck. Bountiful breasts pressed against the yellow cotton. "Guess you haven't heard about the hotel war."

"What hotel war?"

"Right here. That's why the girls are standing out front. See if we can pick up business. There're just too many hotels for a town this size. Two of them have to go."

"Well, a pretty girl is a good way to get customers."

She leaned toward Fargo and said, "You ask for Room Sixteen. I'll be in there waiting."

"Is this part of the service?"

She winked. "Just every once in a while. When the spirit moves me, let's say."

Fargo checked into the hotel, asking for Room Sixteen. The desk clerk winked at him. Fargo was always annoyed by people who winked.

He found his room well-kept, with fresh sheets on the bed, a fresh flower in a narrow vase next to a washbasin uncorrupted by rust, and a selection of six magazines for his reading pleasure. There was a nice hooked rug on the floor and an even nicer rocking chair next to the window.

But nicest of all was the brunette waiting in bed for him. "I'll bet you're tired."

"I am. But I expect there are ways I can be revived."

No other series has this much historical action!

THE TRAILSMAN

Available wherever books are sold or at
www.penguin.com

SIGNET

Charles G. West

**"RARELY HAS AN AUTHOR PAINTED THE
GREAT AMERICAN WEST IN STROKES SO
BOLD, VIVID AND TRUE."
—RALPH COMPTON**

EVIL BREED

0-451-21004-2

The U.S. Army doesn't take kindly to civilians
killing their officers—even in self-defense. But
Jim Culver has two things in his favor: the new .73
Winchester he's carrying—and the ability to use it.

DEVIL'S KIN

0-451-21445-5

Jordan Gray is hunting down his family's killers.
But when he crosses paths with a ruthless posse,
Jordan learns that he doesn't have to take the law
into his own hands to wind up an outlaw.

Available wherever books are sold or at
www.penguin.com

S805

SIGNET HISTORICA

Ralph

JA   02-6
Jacl
dea   Barly
can

JU   96-9
A p
law   man,
how   a
mad

BO   15-8
The   most
diff
Cor   ed
outl   gs.

BL   76-2
Bou   arshal
Har   ano-a-
mar

DE   4-1
The
wer
thou

www.penguin.com

S909